MARS
YEAR ONE
Missing!

BRAD STRICKLAND and **THOMAS E. FULLER**

Aladdin Paperbacks
New York London Toronto Sydney

For Neil and Colin Butler

First Aladdin Paperbacks edition October 2004

Copyright © 2004 by Brad Strickland and the Estate of Thomas E. Fuller

ALADDIN PAPERBACKS
An imprint of Simon & Schuster
Children's Publishing Division
1230 Avenue of the Americas
New York, NY 10020

Designed by Felicity Erwin
The text of this book was set in Simoncini Garamond.

Printed in the United States of America

10 9 8 7 6 5 4 3 2 1

The Library of Congress Control Number 2003116539
ISBN 0-689-86401-9

MARS
YEAR ONE
Missing!

CHAPTER 1

Sean Doe found two things hard to take about his new home. It was too crowded, and yet at the same time, it was too lonely. The colony on Mars was home to several thousand people, but only twenty of them were under twenty-one years old. Sean was fifteen, and sometimes he almost wished he were back on Earth.

Not often, though, and not even when the work was the hardest and the most boring. He was sweating heavily as he worked in one of the greenhouses that provided the colonists with vegetables. The plants grew on mesh screens, their roots spread out and constantly fed with dripping water. The water, the booster lights, and the heater made the greenhouses the warmest and most humid environment on the planet.

Sean had been setting out soybean seedlings. He paused to wipe the stinging sweat out of his eyes—in the low gravity of Mars it crept slowly, even more annoying than it would have been on Earth. The greenhouse dome was so large that he had the illusion of being the only person in it, though he knew Sam Mackenzie and Dan Cross, two of the colony's botanists, were in here somewhere among all the plants with at least two other volunteer workers. "Hot," Sean grunted to no one, and then resumed his job. He fleetingly wondered what was happening back—well, not home. This was home. But what was happening back on the planet where he'd been born.

That was a mystery to everyone on Mars. Marsport had not received a beamcast from Earth for more than five months now. The colonists on Luna, Earth's moon, kept in constant touch and reported that the collapse on Earth seemed to have come from an economic crisis, a rash of wars, outbreaks of disease, and natural disasters that had all peaked at the same time. The Lunatics, as they liked to call themselves, had decided to ride it out. They could do so without much worry— the international Luna colony was over fifty years old, sprawling, well established, and self-sufficient.

The story on Mars was different. The Martian colonists were not quite there yet, not ready for the ties to Earth to be cut. But literally overnight they had determined to stick it out on Mars, to try to become independent. The results included food and water rationing, absolute cooperation, and work. Hard work. Grueling work. Work that left Sean and all his friends exhausted, yearning for sleep, grainy-eyed, and foggy-minded.

A day on Mars was a little longer than an Earth day—about thirty-seven minutes longer—but that meant nothing when you considered that the twenty kids in the Asimov Project had to put in six hours a day in school and then eight hours at work. That left eight hours for sleeping and two hours for meals. The extra thirty-seven minutes, they joked, was for recreation and social life. It wasn't enough.

But the discomforts and the inconveniences didn't mean much to Sean. He was where he belonged, where he'd fought to be, and he would take whatever Mars threw at him. Sean finished his planting and gasped deep lungfuls of the moist air. At first that had been a great novelty on arid Mars. Now, though, he was used to it and found the humidity more an annoyance than anything else.

He mopped his face with a towel and looked around again at the crops growing without any soil at all: potatoes nearly as big as his head, beans, corn—American corn, maize—tomatoes, and other vegetables. The greenhouse let in the weak light of the sun, and solar and wind-powered generators supplied power to the booster lamps, so the greenhouses were about the brightest places on Mars. After a few hours in one, Sean's eyes began to ache, itch, and burn. At least his shift was almost over.

Sam MacKenzie, the director of Greenhouse 7, came over smiling and clapped him on the shoulder. "Good day's work, Sean. Planting's done now in this greenhouse. Good news—we've passed production already, and we have two days' harvest left. You'll be picking beans tomorrow."

"Great," Sean said with a tired smile. Production was the minimum level for survival. Every vegetable over the production level meant a little breathing space, a little edge. No one on Mars was gaining weight, because the food rationing meant that each person received just the level of calories he or she needed to live and work. On the other hand, Mars had a low gravity, so everyone weighed only a third of Earth normal, anyway. Sean's first weeks on Mars had been spent largely learning how to walk without bouncing up into the air or lurching into the walls.

Sean plodded through the passageways connecting the greenhouse to his dorm. He couldn't help yawning, his mouth opening so wide that he could hear the creak of his jaw joints. Farming was hard work, even when the plants grew dangling from nets, their roots bathed in a constant flow of nutrient-enriched water.

Water. That was another problem for the struggling Martian colony. Sean had never really appreciated the availability of water on Earth. It took care of itself: Water vapor rose from the oceans, lakes, and rivers, formed clouds, and the clouds showered rain and snow back down. Water was just there, never in critically short supply.

But Mars had no water cycle. The surface had no

available water at all, except at the Poles, and that was in the form of ice. All the water on Mars had seeped down far below the surface eons ago. Much of it had combined with minerals, including iron, and was locked up in rust, which had given Mars its famous red coloring. Some water remained as permafrost, and when Marsport had been founded to the south of the great volcano Olympus Mons, one reason for the site had been that deep pockets of permafrost had been discovered there. But deep wells had drained the accessible supply, and now no more remained.

The water the colony had was endlessly recycled. However, nothing could prevent a slow, steady loss as water vapor escaped whenever a work crew went onto the surface or through slow oxidation of materials within Marsport itself.

At the rate they were going, Dr. Simak said, the colony was more likely to die of thirst than to starve. Dr. Amanda Simak was the executive director of Marsport and also Sean's legal guardian—if Earth legality meant anything anymore. She was a stern-faced woman who never showed favoritism, and

Sean didn't see nearly as much of her as he would have liked. She was also the one who made the hardest decisions on the planet. And she had just made one that Sean knew would cause a lot of argument.

He was right. Jennifer Laslo, an active, intense blonde girl about Sean's age, was pacing the common room of Sean's dorm wing, waving her arms and sputtering. Two of Sean's friends, eighteen-year-old Patrick Nakoma and fourteen-year-old Alex Benford, were sitting at the table. Alex rolled his eyes as Sean came in. "We know, we know," he said to Jenny as Sean sank into a chair. "But what can we do?"

"There's got to be *something*," Jenny insisted. "Tighter rationing, or speeding up the pipeline, or something! I mean, Lake Ares is *sacred*. It's the only body of water on the whole planet! And it's full of fish!"

"It isn't *full*," Patrick objected. "There aren't enough fish to harvest any for food."

"But they have a right to live, to establish themselves!" Jenny said, red-faced. "Sean, you tell them!"

Sean held up his hands. "Whoa, whoa. I came in late. Are you talking about using the water from Lake Ares for drinking?"

"Of course I am!" Jenny said. "And not just for drinking, but for hydroponics and washing and—it isn't time! We were supposed to do that in three or four years, after we'd created more lakes. Look, Lake Ares is a stable environment right now, but if we draw it down, we're throwing everything off balance. We could kill all twenty species of fish, and if they go, there'll never be any more. Sean, you've got to persuade Dr. Simak to hold off—"

"I can't persuade her to do anything," Sean said. "But aren't you getting ahead of yourself? I heard the announcement a few hours ago, while I was working. The council has said that if the pipeline can't be completed in a month, we'll start taking some water from Lake Ares, that's all. There's still a chance."

"So you're taking her side!" Jenny raged. "How can the pipeline be finished in a month? There are all the warming and pumping stations to bring online, and there are kilometers and kilometers of pipe to get into place, and . . . and . . . it's just not going to happen!"

Alex, a muscular, cheerful young man of African descent, shook his head. "You can't say that. Look, I've flown over a lot of the pipeline. It's more complete than you think. I'd say there's at least a fifty-fifty chance."

"And besides," Patrick put in, "even if the pipeline can't be finished for, oh, six months, we won't make that much of a difference in Lake Ares. We may lower it by a few meters, but there's a lot of water in there."

"That's what they used to think on Earth," Jenny said, her voice shaking with anger. "And where are all the elephants now, huh? And the mountain gorillas, and the giraffes? Extinct in the wild, every one of them! I thought Marsport was supposed to be a new beginning, a way of living with the planet instead of living off it like some kind of parasite!"

Alex had taken out his belt computer and unfolded it. He tapped away at the keyboard. The room darkened as he entered a command, and above the table a holographic display glowed into life: the globe of Mars. It hung there, translucent, as a yellow line sketched itself southward from the base of Olympus Mons, zigzagging its way across plains and hills. It split into four branches. Three of them snaked their way toward ancient volcanoes lying south and east of the colony: Ascraeus, Pavoni, and Arsai. South of Arsai, a lonely thread wound its way across the plain of Daedalia and the uplands of Aonia and Argentium, terminating near the southern polar cap.

"Look," Alex said, working at his keyboard. "There's permafrost at the bases of the three volcanoes. If we can tap into just one deposit, that will buy us time. And if we can get the Schmidt station working, we don't have to worry for hundreds of years. There's plenty of ice there, and more comes in every day!"

"I know about the Bradbury Project, thank you," Jenny said. "But the Schmidt station is a long way from here, and anything could happen. An ice meteorite from Ganymede could smash into the pipeline, or—"

"Not possible," Patrick cut in. "The trajectory is so

flat that ninety-nine percent of the incoming meteorites flash into vapor high in the atmosphere. A few falling chunks of ice won't destroy the whole station."

"But it isn't working yet!" Jenny yelled. "And what if we get along so well by using water from Lake Ares that the council decides we have plenty of time? Things go wrong! You know that things always go wrong!"

Sean felt goose bumps on his arms. He had begun life as one of the few survivors of a terrible biological terrorist act. He had later spent years as a wild kid roaming the streets and underground tunnels of old New York. Somewhere along the line he had picked up a talent. Sean could almost instinctively estimate the chances of something going wrong. A sense of doom had led him to beg Dr. Simak to make room for him in the Mars colony, and that sense had been proved right when Earth suddenly fell out of touch with the colonists. Sean had looked at the pipeline proposals too—and he had to side with Jenny.

Every instinct in him told him that, yes, something was bound to go wrong.

Still, the argument was not something Sean could settle then and there. He was bone-weary, and when Jenny continued to rage about boys and their stupidity, he just went into his room, closed the door, and collapsed onto his bed.

Another thing that was rationed on Mars was space. The materials that made up most of the colony had been prefabricated on Luna and sent to Mars years ago. That meant that all the bedrooms were built exactly alike, small but packed with hidden essentials. The bed folded down from one wall. An electronic center in the opposite wall could show movies or television—though the colonists now had only their own homegrown programs, since Earth was off-line—or could play music, become a computer console, or serve a dozen other functions. The room was so small that, lying in bed, Sean was able to reach out with his foot and touch the screen.

Still, it was his, a room of his own. It had been bare and sterile when he'd first moved in, but little by little

Sean had been putting his stamp on it. One wall now had photos of himself and Amanda when they lived back on Earth, along with an interactive map of Mars, pictures of Alex at the controls of a Martian airplane, and a picture of Jenny laughing. And the room had fallen into the normal disorder that Sean lived in. His clothes weren't stored neatly in a closet, but spread out across the floor so he could dress efficiently.

Sean sniffed. The room even smelled like him.

Showers were rationed too. You got two showers a week, and if you couldn't soap up and rinse off in two minutes, you had to scrape suds from your hide with a towel and spend the next few days feeling itchy. All Marsport was beginning to smell of human sweat.

Sean drifted into a deep sleep. He usually dreamed, often bad dreams of the old days on Earth when he'd stalked, killed, and eaten rats, or elusive dreams of his parents, who had died before he'd really known them. In recent weeks, though, he had always fallen into bed so tired that he couldn't remember any dreams at all.

His stomach woke him after some hours. He hadn't

bothered to eat, and in the dead of night he woke up hungry. He looked at the screen at the foot of his bed, his eyes bleary. Three hours until he had to get up and get ready for school.

He rolled out of bed and went barefoot out into the common room. No one was there at this time of night. He went to the mess unit—a room identical to his dorm room, except that it was taken up with food storage and a heating unit. He pulled a tray from a dwindling reserve of Earth food. It was flat and loosely sealed in a special foil. Sean didn't even read the label, just popped it into the heating unit.

While the food was cooking, he got a glass and slid it into the drink dispenser. He hesitated, then selected plain water. Two hundred and fifty milliliters poured into the glass. That was the full allotment for one meal.

The tray popped out looking puffier. The food had been rehydrated and heated, and when Sean peeled the foil off, he discovered he was eating pizza, with a dessert of hot apples. The aromas of cinnamon and tomato sauce drifted up. They smelled better than he did, anyway.

As Sean munched the pizza, he reflected that it was probably about the last Earth food he would eat. The last supply ship from Earth had given the colony six months of supplies, but some of those had been placed into long-term storage in case of emergencies, and the growing self-sufficiency of the colony meant that for six days out of the week, the colonists could eat homegrown foods. Soon they would be doing that seven days a week.

Just as well, Sean thought. The pizza was too chewy, and it tasted less like pizza than like a pizza box—cardboard-y, bland, without any real zest. Still, he ate every bite. You didn't waste food in Marsport.

The apple dessert was better, though the rehydrated apples had the consistency of mush. Sean saved about half his water for the end of the meal, and he sat sipping it thoughtfully. There were so many things he had always taken for granted back on Earth. Water, of course, but also basic things like, well, like air. The Martian atmosphere was too thin to support life, except perhaps at the very bottom of the deepest part of the Mariner Valley. Even there, you'd gasp like someone at the top of one of Earth's highest mountains. And of course you'd freeze—Mars was cold, and only very gradually getting warmer.

The Bradbury Project was part of the effort to terraform Mars, to make it more like Earth. Far away on Ganymede, one of the larger moons of Jupiter, a giant robotic machine tirelessly scooped up water ice, shaped it into projectiles, and fired it with a mass-driver into space. The ice bullets whipped around Jupiter and spiraled inward toward the sun on a long orbit that took years. At the end, they were captured by the gravity of Mars and entered into orbit around the planet—orbits designed to break down so that after a few passes, the masses of ice came whipping through the air, the heat of entering the atmosphere stripping them into vapor and ice crystals.

The ice meteors did two things. First, they made the air of Mars thicker and richer, allowing it to trap more heat from the sun and to warm the surface. One day, if the plan went as it should, the air of Mars would be thick enough to breathe.

The other thing, of course, was to supply more water to a very dry planet.

Sean finished his drink. He used the table's built-in computer to recall the hologram Alex had displayed.

There was Mars, and there, in glowing yellow, was the pipeline on which the colony depended. It was like a vital artery in the human body. If it failed to function, the colony would die.

Sean had a bad feeling about the pipeline. He couldn't say he was convinced it would never work, but he was afraid that the pressure of time was too great, that the colonists desperate for water would make vital mistakes.

Sitting alone in the dark, thinking of his friend Jenny and her despair and anger, Sean made a decision. Whatever happened with the pipeline project, he had to be part of it. He had spent far too much of his life on his own.

Now, more than anything else, Sean wanted to belong.

CHAPTER 2

"Have you got time?"

Amanda Simak turned at the sound of Sean's voice. Her tired, lined face creased into a smile. "Time for what?"

"For a talk." Sean caught up with her. He had waited in the passageway near her room, hoping to catch her on her way to the Administration offices. "Jenny's worried about the water in Lake Ares."

"We all are." Amanda crinkled her nose and picked at Sean's messy hair. Most of the colonists wore their hair short, but he had let his grow. "Sean, I wish you'd try to be a little neater. I know it's hard to stay clean, but—"

Sean shrugged. "I'm on today's shower schedule. Not much sense before I get in from the greenhouse, though. It's always hot in there. Seriously, is there any alternative to drawing water from the lake?"

They walked side by side, taking up two-thirds of

the narrow passageway. Sean opened all the doors for her—the doors were color-coded to direct colonists to safe areas in the event of a blowout. But all the ones they had to pass were green-coded, meaning the areas had no access to the surface and were safe if an outer part of the colony blew. The doors were heavy, and Sean grunted as he opened each one.

Amanda shook her head. "I've been over it and over it with the hydrologists and the pipeline crew. We can realistically expect some water from the pipeline in a month, if everything goes smoothly. But nothing ever does, does it?"

"Mars has a million ways to kill you," Sean said with a crooked grin, recalling the lesson that had been drummed into his head over and over during his first days on the planet. "Yeah, I know. But how about this? The Asimov Project kids might be able to help with the pipeline construction. We have a two-month school vacation coming up a week from Friday. If we—"

"School breaks are supposed to be for individual study in your field of specialization, not for work-crew duty. And besides, you haven't been trained," Amanda pointed out.

"No, but we don't have to do the skilled work. We can be manual labor. I mean, they need people to check for leaks, to haul equipment, to place blasting charges. Not," he added hastily, "to set them off or anything."

They had reached the Administration dome. It was set up identically to Sean's dorm area or to any of the apartment areas: a cluster of smaller, prefab rooms built around a larger central area. When they stepped into the outer area, Amanda paused, her arms crossed. "Twenty unskilled kids can't do much in two months."

"We can bring the water closer by a day or two," Sean pointed out. "Right now that's pretty important."

Amanda was silent for a long time. Looking at her, Sean thought about how Mars had changed her.

She had always been a fastidious woman, but now she looked as grimy as any of the colonists. Her hair had been cropped close, and her standard uniform of the colony—gray tunic, black slacks—was as rumpled as Sean's. Her face was more deeply lined now, worries and cares dragging the flesh under her eyes into pouches, making her neck muscles sag, even in the low gravity of Mars.

"Maybe," she said at last. "I'll talk to Lt. Mpondo and Dr. Ellman about the idea."

Sean groaned. "Ellman hates me."

Amanda smiled. "No, he doesn't. He's just not sure about the wisdom of having young people here in the colony. He's actually been very impressed with your progress in science and math. He told me so."

Sean didn't respond. Dr. Harold Ellman was a dark-haired, scowling, heavyset man whose expression was a permanent mask of disapproval. He and Tim Mpondo oversaw the education of the twenty Asimov Project students. Sean liked Tim Mpondo, who had a quick wit and a relaxed, easygoing way of encouraging the kids to learn, but Ellman and Sean had rubbed each other the wrong way since day one.

"Don't be so upset," Amanda said, laughing. "Look at it this way: Harold might actually be glad to have his students away from the colony over the break. I'll talk to them about the idea, and I'll ask Elana Moore if she thinks you can make a contribution."

"Who's that?" Sean asked.

Amanda opened her office door. She stood framed in it, a look of surprise on her face. "Elana is the chief design officer on the pipeline project. Young woman, twenty-five, I believe, but a brilliant engineer. Brown hair, brown eyes, about your height. Don't you know her?"

"There are three thousand people here," Sean complained. "I don't know every single one of them!"

"I'll introduce you. Now you'd better run, or you'll be late for school. If you're tardy, Dr. Ellman won't be likely to approve of your plan, you know."

"Thanks." As Sean hurried away to school, something occurred to him that brought a smile to his face. Amanda probably knew every single one of the colonists personally. That was part of her job. And besides, she liked people and trusted them. Sean was working on both of those traits, but sometimes he wondered if he would ever be as gifted and open as

Amanda at dealing with people. He felt so awkward and tongue-tied around strangers, and even with his friends he sometimes had difficulty just talking. Well, mainly with girls. Well, mainly with one girl these days: Jenny.

Sean was cutting it close, and he indulged in a little rule-breaking. He ran in the corridors, as much as you could run on Mars. It was a funny kind of run, almost like skiing without skis, but it was faster than walking.

He got to the school dome and entered just as the chimes went off to signal that class was about to begin. Dr. Ellman was at the central console, his head down, and he didn't notice Sean come in and slip into his desk. Sean, grateful for small favors, looked at his computer screen. Today he had a practice math test, and it looked hard. Jenny, two desks over, was already working at something. Sean began to do the math problems, thinking to himself that today, at least, he'd have something interesting to talk to Jenny about.

They didn't have time to talk until the lunch break. Finals were looming in several units, and since the last school term the students had all lost a little momentum in their studies. Like Sean, they all had jobs. Jenny, who was specializing in adaptive agriculture, worked in the barns—almost a separate colony from Marsport. The colonists were not yet raising animals for meat, but the barn domes held a tiny herd of small cattle, a louder and more troublesome herd of goats, some sheep, some chickens—which had discovered early on that in the low gravity of Mars they could actually fly—and some other farm animals. At this stage in the colony's development, the whole goal was more to make sure that the animals could adapt to a new world than to raise them for slaughter. Jenny helped care for them and was a veterinary assistant during her work shifts.

She was fiercely protective of her animals, even the fish in Lake Ares. Though Sean didn't quite share that urge, he respected Jenny's determined effort to be a vegetarian—well, mostly a vegetarian. She would eat eggs, cheese, and other dairy products.

She preferred to eat alone, usually in the observation dome above the schoolroom. She would sit in a chair, only half her attention on her food, the other half fixed on her portable computer screen. She struggled with history, and she used every opportunity to cram for exams.

She had a salad for lunch, with greens grown on Mars, a sprinkling of cheese made from milk taken from Martian cows, and a chopped hard-boiled egg from a Martian chicken. "You're really going native," Sean said, watching her eat. "You make me feel guilty."

"Why?" Jenny asked, raising one eyebrow. She had very direct, pale blue eyes, eyes that Sean thought could look right through him.

He held up his sandwich. "Earth rations," he said. "Reconstituted chicken, reconstituted tomato, reconstituted lettuce."

Jenny made a face. "And I bet it tastes like reconstituted garbage."

"Pretty close," Sean admitted. "Look, I know how upset you've been over the decision to take water from Lake Ares, and I had an idea that I talked over with Amanda." He briefly filled Jenny in.

She looked hopeful at first, but then she groaned. "Ellman will never let us go. Especially me. My grades fell this term, and he's really been after me to study more."

"Right," Sean said, grinning. "I happen to know that your GPA fell a whole one-one hundredth of a point. Like that's anything. Nickie lost more ground than that, and she's not worried."

"Some people worry more than others," Jenny said with a sniff. "I didn't know that you and Nickie were such good friends."

"Grade-point averages aren't a big secret. Everybody talks about them."

"People who don't have to struggle to get a passing mark in history, maybe."

Sean furrowed his forehead. What was Jenny's problem? Nickie Mikhailova was an outgoing, cheerful girl, and she was a genius at computer design, but she wasn't as friendly with Sean as she was with Jenny. "Have you and Nickie had a fight or something?"

Jenny gave him a dirty look. "Do you think we'd fight about y—about anything?"

"I don't know," Sean said reasonably. "That's why I'm asking. Okay, ax the question. Look, I'll help you study for history. I don't think grades are going to be that much of a problem, anyway. I mean, this is a vital project, and if we don't pitch in, it's going to take even longer. I know they can spare me in the greenhouses for two months, and I think your critters can get along without you for that long, so I really don't think there's a problem. You'd go if you could, wouldn't you?"

Jenny nodded. "I missed the Bradbury Run," she said in a wistful voice. Sean, who had flown down to the edge of the southern polar cap to help set up observation posts that made sure the incoming ice meteors were not straying from their course, didn't say anything. He loved to get out onto the surface of Mars, even if he had to do it wearing a pressure suit, and Jenny did too.

"It'll be fun," he said. He felt a sudden twinge of doubt.

"I'm in, if the teachers give permission," Jenny told him. "Anyway, it was nice of you to ask Amanda about that. Thanks."

Sean nodded. He had oddly mixed feelings. On the one hand, it was good to have Jenny on his side. He had two good friends in Marsport, Alex Benford and Jenny, but of the two, he seemed to have a harder time keeping on Jenny's good side. He enjoyed seeing her smile. On the other hand—well, he wasn't at all sure that volunteering for pipeline duty was the smartest thing to do. Or, for that matter, the safest.

But the class bell chimed, forcing them to hurry down to be on time, and he put his unformed worry completely out of his mind.

2.3

Roger Smith, the youngest person on Mars, had recently celebrated his fourteenth birthday. He kept insisting that that fact made him only *one* of the youngest people on Mars, since Melia Davis was also fourteen, but she pointed out that she would be fifteen in a few weeks, whereas Roger wouldn't turn fifteen for another ten and a half months.

It wasn't the most interesting argument in the world, and Sean was glad when Jenny came to the table to join them, distracting Roger and Amelia. "What a day," Jenny said, collapsing into a chair in the town hall, the largest open area inside the colony. Town hall was a combination recreation room, dining hall, and meeting place, and as usual it buzzed with activity.

"How'd you do?" Sean asked. He didn't have to tell Jenny he was asking how she'd done on her history test.

"Aced it," she said with a broad smile. "A 3.9!"

"Ice!" Melia exclaimed. "I was scared half to death that my history exam would impact, but I pulled out a 3.74. How'd you do it?"

Roger, who had a drawling British accent, said, "Special tutoring, of course. Our Sean is a wizard at history and languages, you know."

"Cut it out," Sean said. "I just helped Jenny memorize a few dates, that's all."

Melia tilted her head. She was short for a fourteen-year-old, and her face had a funny elfin quality with its sharply pointed chin and oddly slanting green eyes. "So Sean, what's the word? Do we go pipelining, or are we anchored here?"

"Search me," Sean said. "Amanda never tells me anything. I know the council has been talking about it, though, and that's why we're all off work rotation this week."

"Really?" Roger asked, raising his eyebrows. "Fancy! I thought it all had to do with them giving us study time. Oh, well, never look a gift holiday in the mouth. Old Earth saying."

"It is not," Melia said, playfully popping him one on his shoulder.

"Ow!" Roger said, wincing. "That's assault, that is!"

A curly-haired, bespectacled boy of seventeen, Mickey Goldberg, spotted them and came over. He was sipping a cup of something or other, probably a milkshake. Mickey had a sweet tooth, and it didn't seem to bother him that the milkshakes didn't contain any real milk or ice cream. Sean found them a pale imitation, but Mickey slurped one down at least once a day. "Hi,"

Mickey said, pulling up a chair. "Mind if I join you?"

Nobody objected. Sean and Mickey hadn't hit it off at first, and sometimes they were still tense around each other, but Sean thought the older boy was really making an effort to be friendlier. "It's on," Mickey said, dropping his voice to a whisper.

"The trip?" Roger asked. "Wicked!"

"How do you know?" Sean asked suspiciously.

Mickey glanced around with exaggerated caution. "Because after I finished my calculus exam, I noticed something had been uploaded into the student computers, some new program suite. It was password protected, but Nickie got it open after only two tries. Guess what it is."

"Hmm—menus for the next term," Roger said. "Bread that tastes almost but not completely unlike real bread, synthetic milk that is to real milk what a boulder is to a cow, and a few good veggies just to keep us drooling."

"No," Mickey said sharply. "Pipeline schematics and a program on how the pumping stations work."

"Ice!" both Jenny and Sean exclaimed together.

"Don't let anyone know I told you," Mickey warned them. "Nickie and I are keeping it a secret, but since Sean dreamed up the idea, I thought you ought to know. But nobody else, okay?"

"Word on that," Melia said solemnly.

And just then Alex Benford weaved his way over to the table, his dark eyes dancing. "Guess what?" he said, making no effort to keep his voice low. "We're going! The school computers have been loaded up with—"

Melia pelted him with a wadded-up napkin, and Roger sprang to his feet and clapped a hand over Alex's mouth. "You know," he said mournfully, "if Marsport didn't have such terrible leaks, we wouldn't have to worry about water!"

It was a bad joke, but everyone at the table laughed at it, anyway—even Alex, who still had Roger's hand clamped on his mouth and sounded as if his head were buried beneath a pillow.

CHAPTER 3

"I'm personally opposed to this, you understand," Dr. Harold Ellman said, his dark scowl sweeping the twenty Asimov Project kids. "You'd be far better advised to remain here in the colony and free up some more seasoned colonists who might actually be of more use on the pipeline project. However, the rest of the council believes that you will benefit from working on the surface. Let me show you the four sites you will be visiting."

Ellman dimmed the lights in the classroom dome and summoned up the same holographic globe of Mars that Sean had seen so many times before. The yellow line still zigzagged across the face of the planet, splitting into four branches. But—Sean squinted to be sure—one of them, the southernmost branch, looked different. He realized that it now made a sharp angle eastward, no longer heading south toward Schmidt Crater and the south pole.

Ellman tapped a remote control, and as he mentioned places on the map, they lit up one by one. Sean could see that now parts of the pipeline, the parts that had been completed, glowed a brighter yellow than the sections that had not yet been joined up.

Ellman fiddled with the control again, and the section showing the colony and the pipeline enlarged, making the details come into sharper focus. The teacher cleared his throat as he highlighted a mountain on the holographic map. "We know for a fact that there are permafrost deposits in the soil on the southern side of Ascraeus Mons." That was the northernmost of a chain of three vast volcanoes, far larger than volcanoes on Earth.

Sean had studied the geology of Mars, and he knew that Mars had no tectonic plate movement, so a volcano that formed on Mars remained right over the hot spot that produced its lava. Sean knew that on Earth, the tectonic plates slowly drifted over the centuries. The Hawaiian Islands were a fine example of that—

the western islands had been built up when they were over the hot spot that sent magma welling up to the surface, but as they drifted to the west, their volcanoes died and new islands were born.

"Do I have to tell you the mechanism that produced the permafrost?" Dr. Ellman asked.

Nickie Mikhailova waved her hand frantically and even before Ellman called on her, she blurted, "The volcanoes outgassed water vapor along with carbon dioxide, nitrogen, and other gases. Millions of years ago, when the volcanoes were active, the atmosphere was thick enough to let the vapor condense into rain or ice. It fell on the slopes of the volcanoes, drained down into the soil, and froze. Below the equator, the southern sides of the volcanoes are the most protected, and the permafrost deposits are closer to the surface there."

"And I thought you knew nothing about any science that didn't have to do with computers," Ellman said in a dry, sarcastic voice. "Broadly correct, Mikailova. The other two volcanoes presumably have similar permafrost deposits. Of course, none of the three is close to the size of Olympus Mons, so the supplies are not likely to be great. But here"—he flicked a key on his remote, and the crooked, curving yellow pipeline off to the south and east glowed brighter on the globe— "yes, here is a fascinating possibility. What is this feature, let me see, ah—Doe?"

Sean leaned forward. The highlight was pulsing red over a long, slanting scar just to the west of the great plateau called Solis Planum, the Plain of the Sun. The whole southern rim of the plateau was fringed with intricate networks of braided channels, evidence that surface water had once flowed on Mars. "That's a valley," he said.

"Rift valley," murmured Jenny, sitting beside him, too softly for Ellman to hear. That was an art that she had picked up early in her education.

"I mean it's, uh, a rift valley," Sean corrected himself.

"You surprise me, Doe," Ellman said. "Quite right. The limited tectonic activity on Mars did open up a number of these valleys. The largest of them is— Goldberg?"

"The Valles Marineris," the older boy replied, his

tone bored, but not quite bored enough to call down the teacher's wrath.

"Yes, correct. However, let's leave that out for now. It's steep-sided and very deep, so we won't be exploring that area for water for some years. The valley we're interested in is not quite so deep, more accessible, and possibly very rewarding. Now, you may be aware that if everything had gone according to plan, the second and larger Martian colony would have been founded on Solis Planum. Why, Smith?"

"Water," Roger Smith said promptly. "Water, water everywhere. Or at least, water, water a hundred meters beneath the surface."

"Accessible water," Ellman droned on. "And, as you say, only about three hundred feet beneath the surface. But this rift valley on the southeastern side of the plateau offers an even more exciting possibility. The atmosphere of Mars is much thicker now than it was a hundred years ago, thanks to our terraforming efforts. At the bottom of the valley, the air pressure is just great enough to allow ice to remain stable, instead of subliming. And what is subliming, Davis?"

Melia always sounded frightened when Ellman called on her. In a squeaky voice, she said, "When ice goes straight to vapor form without melting into water first. It happens at low pressures."

"Very good," Ellman said. His smile came and went fast, like a mousetrap snapping. "The exciting possibility is that at the bottom of the valley, the permafrost may literally be within arm's reach beneath the surface. Some water vapor constantly percolates up from beneath as the deep permafrost sublimes. It's very likely that, with the increasing air pressure, much of the escaping water vapor has refrozen into ice and has remained that way. The problem, of course, is that the extraction unit is far away, down toward the South Pole. But the engineers have been working on that—"

Sean yawned. Ellman was not a very inspiring lecturer, and he went on and on. Sean gathered that the water-extraction installation already built in Schmidt Crater was too massive to break down and move. However, the factory units in the colony were cobbling together a smaller automated water-extraction unit from spare parts and machinery they could adapt to other uses.

Since the pipeline could reach the rift valley in a month and couldn't reach Schmidt Crater for well over a year, it was being diverted. Some of the pipeline crews would be dropped into the bottom of the valley, where they would finish preparing the extraction factory. When the pipeline reached the valley, it would be connected to the factory. The unit would then melt, or partially melt, ice beneath the surface, and then strain out soil and rock particles. The slushy ice then would be sent through the pipeline on a long journey northward to Marsport.

At noon the class broke, and Sean walked back toward the town hall with Alex and Jenny. "Well, that was boring," he said.

"Are you kidding? If we pull this off," Alex replied, "we'll have plenty of water for years. That's about the most exciting news I've heard in ages."

"Alex is right. Think of it! One day Mars will have lakes. Seas," Jenny said, her eyes dancing. She linked her arm through Sean's as they walked. "And you got us a chance to be in on the beginning of it. Thanks, Sean!"

Sean nodded, feeling pleased. In a way, he felt almost as if he had wrapped up hope for the future and had given it to Jenny as a present.

Now if they *could* pull it off . . .

3.2

Elana Moore, Sean decided a few days later, was just as hard a taskmaster as Dr. Ellman. Oh, she was nicer about it, and her jokes didn't have the sarcastic cutting edge that Ellman's did, but she wouldn't let you get away with anything less than your best.

She was about twenty-five, trim and slightly built, with close-cut brown hair and a skier's body. Even in the bright blue pressure suit and helmet, Sean could pick Elana out from the others by the quickness of her movements and by the intensity of her focus. She was the one bustling everywhere, quick to point out a mistake, quick to praise a good job.

They were training just south of Marsport. It was a

clear day, with a deep blue cloudless sky overhead. To the north the jumble of domes, corridors, and greenhouses of the colony glittered in the noon sun. Past that, the huge red bulk of Olympus Mons rose into the sky, looking as if the horizon had somehow warped itself up to an unimaginable height. The twelve-person crew was laying a small pipeline from Marsport to a brand-new oxygen rendering station ten kilometers south of the colony. It was a simple job, but Sean was quickly learning that simple jobs became devilishly complicated when he had to wear gloves and view the world through a helmet.

Still—Sean felt a quiet surge of pride—he was wearing the blue Pathfinder pressure suit at last, not the green Excursion one. The upgrade made him feel more a part of the Martian colony than ever. True, all the Asimov kids now wore the blue suits, not just Sean, but that somehow made the achievement seem even better. They had made it as a team.

Roger Smith didn't seem particularly proud of his blue suit at the moment, though, as he knelt beside the half meter–diameter pipe, securing an impeller unit with a bolt driver. Roger didn't weigh much on Mars, and it was almost comical to watch him. The driver was shaped like a streamlined power drill, and when the bolts began to tighten, the torque made Roger lurch and brace himself. If Roger wasn't careful, Sean thought, he'd be spinning like a top himself, and the bolt would stay frozen in place.

"Blast whoever invented this blasted piece of blasted junk," Roger growled, his voice crackling over Sean's helmet communicator. "These are supposed to be tightened to a torque of a hundred and ten Newton Meter units, and it's still at a hundred and four."

"Let me help," Sean said.

Roger lifted a gloved hand to wave him off. "I want to try one more time. Might as well go into this with some useful skills. Here we go." He bent back to his task, leaned hard, and the thin whine of the torque gun started again, with Roger visibly straining to hold the tool steady against its strong turn. "I think I've got it!"

"Well done, Mr. Smith!" It was Elana. She had

come up from behind Sean, and her crisp voice surprised him and made him jump a little. "Is that the last one?"

"Yes, the last of six bla—blessed little bolts," Roger said, rising carefully from his kneeling position. "And, I hope, the last of the impellers."

"It is. All right, get in the truck. We're going to take a look at the vent dome."

Sean and Roger clambered into the hauler. Jenny was there already, her face looking strained and sweaty through her helmet. "Hard work," she said to Sean.

Sean nodded. It was almost Martian summer now, and the temperature outside the pressure suits was comparatively torrid for this latitude—nine degrees Celsius, or on the old Fahrenheit scale, about forty-eight degrees. Sean's early impression of Mars had been that the planet was a deep-freeze of a world, but warmer weather had made it far more comfortable to stay outside for hours. If the air had been thick enough, he reflected, it would even be possible to roam around in his clothes and a light jacket and still feel relatively warm. As it was, work made him hot—the pressure suits were much more flexible than the ones the first astronauts had worn on their moon landings, but they still had one problem. It was harder to disperse heat in warmer weather than it was to generate it in colder weather. He got very stuffy and sweaty inside a pressure suit.

The truck, one of the long, articulated haulers normally used to carry equipment, joggled, jounced, and jolted over the surface, sending up a fine cloud of red dust behind them. They seemed to roar along, but they were really creeping—maybe thirty kilometers per hour, barely five times faster than a running man. The tired crew chatted a little as they rode out to the dome of the oxygen cracking plant.

Mars was a world whose surface was mostly composed of rust—oxides of minerals and metals. It was possible to extract the oxygen from these compounds, but as Sean had learned, there was no such thing as a free lunch. Separating oxygen from the minerals required lots of energy.

The effort was worthwhile, because in addition to the

oxygen, the process produced carbon and iron, and the two were then processed into steel, but the energy demands were high. Part of the power came from wind-generated electricity, part from microwave energy beamed down from satellites, and part from thermal generators. The oxygen replenished the air in the colony—something they hoped the greenhouses would eventually do. The carbon was essential in producing steel, and the metal the units produced provided a basic building material for the colony. Not a bad bargain, Sean thought, even though it did cost tons of energy.

They reached the dome, a steel half-sphere a few meters across rising from the surface like the back of a tortoise. Most of the machinery was underground. This was just the access to the automated factory, together with the power inputs and the valves that let the gas flow. The crew climbed down from the hauler and Elana opened a control panel on the side of the dome. "All right, here goes. Let's see if this critter will breathe."

She switched the power on. Sean felt a deep vibration rising from his boots, strong enough to make his teeth feel as if they were buzzing. Elana checked the dome's readouts, then hit more switches. "Here goes," she said at last. "Half pressure as a test."

They stared across the Martian plain at the silvery pipeline winding its way toward the distant colony. Suddenly Jenny yelled, "There's a leak!" She pointed a blue-gloved finger into the distance.

Squinting, Sean saw a plume of white vapor. He sighed. The welding in a joint had failed, or an impeller had blown. Elana got a position reading, then shut down the machinery and said, "Board the truck. Let's see what the damage is."

In fact, the damage turned out to be minor. A seam had given way, and a little spot welding took care of it. But Elana sounded far from happy. "This little line is barely ten kilometers long. Multiply that by a factor of a thousand, and you'll have some idea of the job ahead of you. And if we have one blowout in ten kilometers, then on the real thing we could expect a thousand."

"At least," Roger muttered, "my bolts held."

Sean had hoped that he and Jenny would be assigned to the same team, but no such luck. Jenny wasn't as good as he was at the brute-strength requirements of the pipeline job, but she had a touch with measurements and record keeping that snared her the position of first assistant to Elana Moore, and Elana was going to the rift valley southwest of Solis Planum. An advance team was already working there to assemble the water-extraction unit, and Elana was going along to supervise.

Sean, Roger, and Mickey Goldberg were to provide manual labor for the northernmost branch of the pipeline. Early one morning they and a half-dozen older men and women boarded one of the Martian airplanes, a craft with huge wings, and settled in for the flight to the south and east. Training had taught Sean not to expect much in the way of accommodations, and so he was not terribly disappointed to see where he would be living for the next several weeks.

The colonists called them *hootches*. They were

essentially metal-and-plastic tents, shallow domes about ten feet in diameter, radiation-shielded with a built-in air generator and heating unit. Each one could house four people (uncomfortably), and Sean resigned himself to having three roommates for the next month and a half.

The work site consisted of six hootches arranged in a semicircle around an airlock leading into a tunnel blasted into the Martian bedrock. The tunnel housed the collection station. Pipes large enough for a man to crawl through led from the tunnel mouth down into the crust. Long trenches had already been scooped out, and robot drills had reached a rich pocket of permafrost beneath these. The machinery was mostly in place now. What remained was largely a matter of hauling and shoving, making sure that the ice-bearing soil would come smoothly into the processing units in the tunnels and that the extractors would work.

During daytime in the summer, freezing would not be much of a problem, but the temperature dropped sharply at night. All along the pipeline were heating units using fresnel lenses, electric power, and other techniques to keep the water in the pipeline in a slushy, moveable state—a slurry state, as Elana had called it.

Bob Wilbanks, the foreman for Sean's work detail, was a lanky, skinny, humorless man in his late thirties, quiet and apparently laid-back until he suspected one of his team was slacking off. Then he had an astonishing vocabulary.

The days seemed long to Sean. Hours in the pressure suit carrying supplies, testing pipe fittings, and running machinery left him exhausted. The hootch was smelly and cramped. You could stand completely upright only toward the center, and Sean got used to crouching as he headed toward his bed or toward his locker.

The workers had two meals a day, breakfast and dinner, because it was more trouble than it was worth to take off the pressure suits. Water was no problem—they could produce plenty of that, so they had enough to drink. None of the hootches had showers, though, so they tried to make do with sponge baths, though these did little to make Sean feel really clean.

Breakfast was a cold meal: compressed rations of

fruit and carbohydrate-rich "Mars bread" that had the consistency of a bowling ball. At night they ate heated rations that soon began to taste alike, if you could say they had much taste at all. After dinner they played chess or cards, read on their portable computers, or just tried to grab as much sleep as possible. They tested machinery, moved machinery, and serviced machinery. Mickey Goldberg once grunted, "You know, the word *robot* comes from an old Czech word meaning *slavery*. Robots are supposed to work for us, but I'm starting to think the machines are in charge and we're their servants!"

"Things are in the saddle, and they ride mankind," Roger said. "One of your American writers said that. Henry David Thoreau, I think."

"I feel like *something's* been riding me," Sean said with a groan, trying to stretch the kinks out of his aching back. "How much closer are they?"

He didn't have to explain what he meant. The pipeline was creeping toward the collection unit. When the pipeline construction crew reached them, they would see how much water they could send to

Marsport. But they couldn't begin until the connections were made and the line was tested.

"I heard they're seven clicks closer," Mickey said, lying on his inflatable bunk with his forearm thrown across his eyes.

"Seven kilometers a day," Roger said. "Let me see. That means they should be here in ten days' time. Which means two weeks, probably, or longer. There'll be a sandstorm, or a hauler will break down, or they'll damage some sections of pipe. There's one thing you can count on in this blasted place. Something always goes wrong."

Mickey didn't reply. Sean heard him snoring. "He could go to sleep on a meat hook," he said.

"Lucky fellow," Roger replied sourly.

4.1

In their third week of work, Mickey and Sean got chosen to set up a directional beacon on the slopes of Ascraeus Mons. Like almost every volcano on Mars, Ascraeus was a vast dome of hardened lava, rising more than six miles above the surrounding plain. In the hootch, Wilbanks pointed out the spot where the beacon should go, using a large-scale paper map. "When you set the beacon up, be sure you activate the global positioning relay," he said. "That will give the pipeline crew the best bearing. Don't screw up."

"We won't," Mickey said.

"Do it, don't say you'll do it," Wilbanks snapped. His temper was short after months at this advance station, and Sean had learned early that the man had a short fuse. "Take the north trail to the scarp line. You want to position the beacon as high as possible, but don't get too close to the cliffs. There's some unstable rock face that could be a problem."

When all was said and done, Mickey and Sean set out on a climb that would last for about six hours. They took a small rover as far as they could. This was a squat four-wheeled vehicle, no race car, but one that could move faster than a man on foot. The ground underneath tilted, and when the grade became too steep, Sean and Mickey climbed out and started up the trail on foot. Mickey carried the beacon, a small unit on an anchor rod, and three rod extensions. Sean carried a rock drill that would let them set the beacon in secure, solid stone.

"Not much of a trail," Mickey huffed.

Sean had to agree. The trail existed mostly in someone's imagination. A Pathfinder crew had wound its way up, leaving small piles of loose stones as markers. They would find one, look at its base for a line of stones giving them a direction, and set off climbing that way until the next marker came into view. Sometimes they had to drop and scramble on all fours, and sometimes they could make good time standing and walking.

After what seemed like hours, they took a rest break and looked back. They were hundreds of meters above the extraction unit and the construction camp, but not even on the foothills of the volcano. The toehills, Sean thought, was more like it. Though Ascareus was not as huge as Olympus, it was an imposing mountain nonetheless. Sean couldn't imagine climbing all the way to the summit, where rings of ancient craters showed that the volcano had once sent clouds of dust, vapor, and gas blasting into the upper atmosphere of Mars.

Sean and Mickey strained to see if they could glimpse the pipeline, but they couldn't be sure. Hazy clouds made the sunlight dim and milky, and what Mickey insisted was the pipeline could have been just the top of a ridge in the distance. They rose at last and climbed higher.

Gradually they came within view of a scarp, a cliff face. The shield volcanoes of Mars looked deceptively smooth in photos taken from space. Closer in, they offered lots of broken landscape. Here a subterranean collapse had left a sheer cliff that rose perhaps a thousand meters. They were to place the beacon near the foot of the cliff, but not right against it.

They searched for some relatively level ground without much success. "Closer to the cliff base," Mickey suggested.

Sean didn't much like the idea. The foot of the cliff lost itself in a long pile of broken stone—*scree* as David Czernos, the lead aereologist of Marsport, had taught them to call it. The scree was hundreds of meters deep, hills in itself, and was eloquent testimony that the cliff could break apart and thunder down stones on their heads. But Sean had to admit that the slope leveled out considerably closer to the cliff, so reluctantly he followed Mickey.

They compromised on what seemed to be a safe place, not quite level but rising at a fairly constant angle of fifteen degrees or so. The base of the scree was perhaps a hundred meters away from the spot they chose. Sean assembled the drill and started to make the hole while Mickey assembled the anchor shaft.

It was slow work. The drill screeched and spat out a cloud of dust and a constant shower of grainy pebbles. When Sean reached a depth of a meter, he had to pull the drill out and extend the bit, then start again. Regulations called for a two-meter anchor hole, and the beacon rod would slip into that. The beacon itself would be on the part extending above the surface—a minimum of ten meters above, according to their orders.

Mickey finished his assembly job and relieved Sean at the drill. The wind was getting up. Sean, resting, saw that the plume of dust was whipping away to the south. He looked across the plain to the east of the volcano and saw a reddening of the air on the horizon. "Dust storm," he said. "Let's finish up."

Mickey pulled the drill out. "This should be close enough. Help me sink the shaft."

As if they were raising a flagpole, Sean and Mickey pushed the long shaft of the beacon up, fitted the bottom into the hole they had drilled, and dropped it in. Sean checked a portable transceiver to make sure the beacon was operating correctly. Then they heard Wilbanks's urgent voice on their helmet radios: "Beacon team! Do you read?"

"Goldberg here," Mickey said. "We've finished, boss."

"Get back to camp. The pipeline crew's battened down on the trail. There's one big sandstorm approaching. Hurry!"

It took them a few minutes to break down the drill, and then they started down the trail with Mickey carrying the drill body and Sean the long bits. Sean stopped suddenly and said, "What's that?"

Mickey looked back at him. "What do you mean?"

"Vibration," Sean said.

Mickey looked up at the cliff, off to their right. "Landslide! Let's get out of here!"

Sean never knew whether their drilling had been enough to upset some fragile balance or if the rising wind had played some part. What was clear was that a fifty-meter stretch of cliff high over their heads had broken loose and was cascading down. Boulders the size of cars tumbled end over end, and a shower of dust and smaller debris rode down the cliff like an avalanche of stone.

A falling boulder the size of Sean's head smashed onto the trail ahead of them, bounced impossibly high in the weak gravity, and bounded on down the slope. Mickey stumbled and fell, dropping the drill and landing on his face and stomach. Sean heard him curse. "I've cracked my faceplate!"

Sean fumbled at his belt. Every colonist carried an emergency repair kit, and he pulled his out. "Turn over so I can get to it!"

Mickey was gasping frantically. "I'm losing air! I'm gonna die!"

"Ax that!" Sean yelled. "Turn over! I'm getting a patch!"

Mickey rolled to his side in a spasmodic jerk. He tried to clamp his hands against his faceplate, but Sean tugged them away. Sean could see Mickey's terrified eyes, wide behind their round spectacles.

The crack jagged diagonally from about the height of Mickey's left eye down to the center of the faceplate. The warm, humid air from the suit was squealing out, jetting into visible white steam in the low pressure. "I can fix it," Sean said. He found a sheet of pliotape, clumsily peeled off the backing, and smoothed it over the break. "That get it?"

Mickey's voice was taut. "I can still hear a hissing.

Slowed it, though." He took three deep breaths, then groaned as he got to his feet, his legs shaking. "Let's go before I run out of air."

The worst of the landslide had been behind them. Sean glanced back and saw that at least the beacon had not taken a direct hit, though loose fallen stones lay all around its base. They had not reached the rover before Mickey had to switch to his reserve oxygen tank, and they got back to camp just before that ran out. By then the whole eastern horizon had vanished in a roiling cloud of dust and sand. Mickey and Sean had expected to be bawled out, but Wilbanks just ushered them into the hootch with a hasty word of advice: "Settle in. Looks like a big one."

4.2

It was a three-day blow. Sean thought he would go crazy. All day and all night the hootch screeched as a billion fingers of sand dragged across it with a sound like dentist's drills. No one could go outside into the blinding storm. The flying dust would abrade a pressure suit's faceplate, would get into joints and crevices and foul the servos that made it possible to breathe and live. Sean had been through some dust storms back in Marsport, days when it seemed the sun had not even risen and everything was a midnight rage of chaos. But it was one thing to hunker down with three thousand other people and another to be trapped in a tiny metal dome with only three others.

The wind let up on the third day, and by the late afternoon they were able to go out and survey the damage. The eastern side of the hootch, fortunately the one opposite the airlock, was buried in a dune of dust that curved around each side of the dome in a broad crescent. They had to dig out the extraction-unit hatch—it was buried under six feet of dust that had collected against the face of the rise. But everything was still working, and before nightfall Wilbanks picked up the pipeline crew on the radio. They were eighteen kilometers away, ready to resume work.

Four days later, Roger let out a whoop as he stood staring off to the east. "There they are!"

Sean hurried over to join him. In the distance he saw the glitter of sun on a moving object, one of the haulers. "Great," he said. "I'll be glad when they get here."

"You worry too much," Roger said. "I think they told you about one time too often that Mars can kill you."

Sean said, "It's not that. It's just that I'll be glad to see the pipeline connected at last." But in fact he had been worried. Overland travel on Mars was always dangerous. He joined the others in welcoming the incoming team members.

Wink Crandall was the leader of the pipeline team. She was in her twenties and had been a pilot when she had first arrived at Marsport four years earlier, but in the intervening time she had developed a skill with machinery. "Ran out of pipe sections two weeks ago, and Marsport had some trouble ferrying more to us," she said. "Otherwise we would've been here sooner. Well, another day of hard work should do it. I hope you guys are ready to head home, because I'm sick of roughing it!"

The team at the extraction unit became pipe layers too. They dug and blasted a trench, fitted together sections of pipeline, and bolted sensor and impeller units at the proper intervals. When the pipe team came in from the east, they found that the last section required very minor adjustment. The two parts of the pipe joined together, and someone weakly cheered.

"Ought to have a golden spike," Roger Smith said.

Mickey Goldberg gave him a long look. "What are you talking about?"

"Your American history. When a railroad was built from the Atlantic to the Pacific, the last part of it was driving in a golden spike. That happened in 1969. Or maybe 1869. Primitive times, anyway."

Bob Wilbanks said, "Forget the golden spike. I'll be satisfied if this thing produces water. I might drive an icicle in if it does."

It took another few hours to finish all the preparation, and then everyone, the pipeline crew and the extraction-unit crew, crowded into the tunnel that housed the main machinery. The air seemed thin—it was a slightly richer oxygen mix than in the hootches, but at a slightly lower pressure—and there was hardly room to turn around. Sean stood at the rear of the crowd, his spine pressed against the rough stone of the tunnel wall.

Bob Wilbanks stood at the control unit up front. "Well, I won't make a speech. And I don't have a golden spike, Roger. But if this thing works, I'll be happy."

He switched the extraction unit into pump mode. Machinery whined into action, and after a few minutes Sean heard a definite sound of gurgling. Everyone stood tensely, waiting for some word from Wilbanks.

At last the skinny man smiled. "The slurry has hit the first sensor unit five clicks out. We're in business. Ladies and gentlemen, let's go home."

4.3

There was something sad about leaving the advance base. Sean had no love for the dark, smelly hootch, and the work had been as hard as anything he had done in his life, but the weeks of close contact with Roger and Mickey had given him a better understanding of both of them. All the kids in the Asimov Project were orphans—that way, as someone had explained to Sean, if they were lost, at least there wouldn't be any grieving parents back on Earth. Some, like Sean, couldn't even remember their parents. Others, like Roger, had lost their parents when they were seven or eight years old.

Sean now thought that Roger's offhand joking style, his tendency to see everything as a punch line, hid an underlying sadness. Occasionally the British boy would have what he called "a case of the silence," when he just didn't want to talk or be around anyone. Sean suspected that Roger was thinking of his parents at such moments and missing them terribly.

Mickey Goldberg was another story. He was fiercely competitive and tended to insist that things be done his way. Sean had always thought of Mickey as a genius, good at everything. Now he began to understand that Mickey was afraid of failure. Marsport was the closest thing to home that Mickey had ever known, and he fiercely wanted not only to belong, but to be an indispensable part of it.

As for Sean, well, he was coming to understand himself a little better too. His first few years had been spent in a research institute run by the United States government. He had survived a deadly biological attack, and the scientists and doctors had wanted to know what allowed his system to resist the terrorists' germ attack. The people who had raised him hadn't been cruel, but they hadn't been particularly loving, either. Sean had been treated somewhat like an unusually intelligent lab animal, a hamster that could talk well but that had no real feelings, none that the experimenters needed bother with, at any rate. Then, after a horribly failed time with an unsuitable foster family, Sean had spent years living a feral life on his own, like a hunted animal.

Now he was starting to learn what friendship was, and family. And he was deeply fearful of losing what he had gained. He found it hard to open up to others, but he was trying.

Sean caught himself and stopped his brooding—that was what Jenny called it when he fell silent and started thinking about his own past. The present was enough to think about. By contrast to the days of hard work at the base, the days following completion of the work were, well, boring. The colony could spare only one plane to bring all the work crews back to Marsport. By common consent, they all agreed that the ones who had been away the longest should be the first ones to return. That left Sean, Roger, and Mickey in the last dozen, and so they had to wait for several days while the plane ferried everyone else back home. The last couple of days were a strain. The hootch wasn't crowded any longer, not after Wilbanks' departure. They had no more work to do, so they luxuriated in doing nothing, lying in their bunks and reading, eating the tasteless rations, and talking about what they wanted to do next.

"I'm taking a shower," Roger said. "And I'm going to insist on four full minutes of water. I've earned that!"

"I'm going to get new lenses for my glasses. These

somehow got all scratched." Mickey took the glasses off and squinted through them. He was one of only half a dozen people on Mars who wore glasses. Most of the colonists had perfect vision, either naturally or through surgery, but Mickey's problem with his vision was one of the rare type that could not be surgically corrected. The same machine that created new lenses for instruments made his specs, and though he often complained about them, he needed them to see well. He put the glasses back on and squinted through them. "Ugh. These are so scratched it's like looking through fog. Anyway, as soon as these are fixed, I'm going to get in some apprentice time."

"You've *had* apprentice time, Goldberg," Roger said, yawning. "You're hydraulics, and this has been one long experiment in the movement of water."

"It's a little too practical for my taste," Mickey said. "I want a few weeks of nice quiet theory. And I'd give my right arm for a milkshake."

"Me, I'd give my right arm to be ambidextrous," said Roger, and he ducked as Mickey threw a pillow at him.

They took the last flight to Marsport the next day. Sean had a window seat, and he watched the harsh, oddly beautiful landscape of Mars drift past. At some points they could see sections of the pipeline. Most of the distance it ran underground, but occasionally short, insulated sections of it had to pass over a gully or run along the crest of a ridge. It gleamed in the sun, and Sean couldn't help feeling proud of having played a part in constructing it, at least in a small way.

They landed, got back to their dorm wing, and took their showers. Despite Roger's determination, they were still limited to just two minutes, but they were a glorious two minutes for Sean, who felt as if he were sluicing off an inch-thick layer of grime. They rattled around then, the only three in a dorm wing equipped for five.

They ate some real food, and when they had finished, Sean said, "I'm going to Comm to try to call Jenny. I want to see how she's doing way down there in the valley."

"Tell her hello for me," Roger said.

Sean saw the corridors of Marsport with new eyes. What had once seemed cramped now was positively spacious, at least in comparison to the advance base. To enter a room where twenty or more people could mill about freely seemed like finding wide open spaces. And Marsport no longer seemed to stink of sweat. After spending several hard-working weeks in one pressure suit, Sean thought the air in Marsport was almost fragrant.

No one he knew was on duty in the communications center, a dome crammed with radio and microwave equipment, but a youngish communications tech put him through to the Plain of the Sun center. There was a slight hitch to the transmissions, because Mars had no ionosphere to bounce radio waves off, and all transmissions had to go from the surface to one satellite to the next, then back down. It gave voices a tinny, distant quality.

Jenny sounded thrilled when she finally came online. "Sean! How's it going?"

"It's *gone,*" he said cheerfully. "Advance Base One is pumping slush. We beat it here, but in the next day or so, Marsport will get its first sip of water from the pipeline. How's it there?"

"Hard work," Jenny said. "You should see the way down into the valley. Switchback road. You have to travel about twenty clicks to get ahead two clicks, the road winds so much. And the bottom of the valley is, like, mush. Soil that clumps like snow. But it's great. There's ice all over the place here! When we get connected, Marsport will be okay for water for the next fifty years."

Sean took a deep breath. Fifty years. Fifty. Marsport was less than ten years old. All along the goal had been to discover whether a human settlement could endure for one Martian year—six hundred and eighty-seven Earth days—without outside assistance from Earth. No one had seriously expected that the colonists would spend the rest of their lives on Mars.

"Sean?"

"Yeah, great!" Sean said. "Look, I'm stealing time on the comm net. I'd better let you go. Say hi to Alex for me. Hope to see you soon!"

Jenny said something that he didn't quite catch, and

then the conversation was over. Sean left the center feeling strangely depressed. Something, he thought, was wrong somewhere. He didn't know just what.

But that gift, or curse, of his was kicking in. He had the feeling that something bad was going to happen, and soon.

He wished he had some idea of what it might be.

5.1

The water from Ascraeus station began to arrive in Marsport. It came in as slush, which had to be processed to make it liquid and drinkable, but it did come flowing in. The hydrologists estimated that the amount being pumped in from the first remote station barely balanced the average loss of water from the colony. As Roger put it, the first pipeline wouldn't let the colonists go for a swim, but it would keep them from dying of thirst.

Days passed, and Sean began to feel at home again, though a strange kind of apprehensiveness walked everywhere with him. Part of his uneasiness was in not having more friends his age. He, Roger, and Mickey were temporarily the only teens in Marsport, and they had seen plenty of each other on the work detail. All the other Asimov Project kids were out on pipeline duty—and when Sean complained about that to Amanda, she tartly reminded him that the whole thing had been *his* idea, after all.

Then, one week to the day following Sean's return, a plane brought an injured Nickie Mikhailova in from the Arsai Mons base. She had caught her leg in a crevice and had a bad fracture above her left ankle.

Sean went to see her in the hospital dome the day she arrived. She was the only patient—the Marsport colonists had been carefully screened for communicable diseases, vaccinated for every possible infection, and given overall health screening before leaving Earth. Marsport had no problem with infectious diseases, only with accidents like Nickie's or with disorders that colonists might develop after arriving on Mars, like heart disease or cancer, against which there were no vaccines. Fortunately, so far no one had developed any serious problems.

Nickie was sitting up in bed, looking grumpy. Her leg lay immobilized in a lightweight cast, and she rolled her eyes when Sean came into her room. "Call me clumsy," she said. "It was all my own stupid fault.

Shouldn't have tried to carry something I couldn't see over, but I thought I could make it."

"It's okay," Sean said with a smile. "I'm not blaming you. What happened?"

Nickie shrugged. "I was carrying a short section of pipe, about two meters long. We needed just enough to connect the end of the pipeline to a heating junction. Well, you know me: Russian peasant type, right? I figured that I could easily lift a piece of pipe that on Earth would weigh a hundred kilos, because here it's only about a third of that. I did lift it, too, but I couldn't see where I was going and stuck my foot in a crack. I fell forward, and I heard a snap, and then I hurt like blazes."

"Sorry. That kind of thing could happen to anyone, though, so don't beat yourself up over it. How long are you going to have to wear that thing?"

"The cast?" Nickie wrinkled her pug nose. "Six whole weeks. Everybody's going to want to know what happened, and there's no way to lie to them, so everyone in school will think I'm some kind of idiot. And imagine me hopping around on crutches. Bull in a china shop, right? Oh, well, at least I'll have an excuse to be late when school starts again. So catch me up. How did your tour go?"

They were both hungry for company, and they talked for a long time. Then Sean played a couple of games of chess with her. They weren't much fun for him, because Nickie was a real chess shark. She'd memorized all sorts of classic games, and she seemed to have the irritating ability to see forward in time, guessing exactly what Sean was going to do with his bishops, knights, and rooks. Both games ended pretty quickly with Sean getting caught in a checkmate he didn't see coming.

"Want any movies or anything?" Sean asked.

"Got a direct feed to the vid library through the hospital net, thanks," Nickie said with a smile. "Thanks for not making fun of me fouling up this way. Boy, I hope I'm not the only one who fouls up." She looked appalled the second she said that and then rushed on: "I didn't mean that the way it came out. I don't really want anything bad to happen to any of the others. It's just that I hate being the one who—you know."

"I know," Sean said. "Hey, Mickey and I almost brought a mountain down on our own heads." He told her about the adventure, making it seem a lot less dangerous and a lot more amusing than it had felt at the time. One of the medical staff brought in Nickie's lunch, and Sean left her alone to eat it. He wandered restlessly, reflecting that it was nice to talk to Nickie, but somehow it wasn't the same as talking with Jenny.

He spoke to Jenny again later that afternoon by radio. She said the extraction unit was working after a fashion, but only at forty percent efficiency. The engineers were trying to figure out what was wrong, and until they could do that, nothing much was going on. Meanwhile, Jenny said, the work had been hard, everyone was stinky, and she was getting really homesick for some actual organic food, not the processed stuff in the silvery ration packs.

"Some of us are going to go on the pipeline trail later," Jenny said. "There's not much for us to do here, and the heating and impeller junctions have to be preset. Six of those left to do on this end, so the boss is going to pick a volunteer crew to go out with tents and stuff and spend about two weeks setting up the junctions."

"Don't volunteer," Sean said without even thinking.

"Too late," Jenny's voice crackled back. "Already did it. Look, I'm getting cabin fever here. Hootch fever. I'm sick of being stuck here with not enough to do, anyway."

"I don't like the thought of your being out on the plateau with nothing but tents," Sean said. "We had a bad storm when we were at the advance base. Something like that would pick up a tent and sail it away like a paper plate in a high wind. You wouldn't have a chance."

"We're not taking chances," Jenny replied, sounding cantankerous. "We've all had the basic training. Anyway, they'll wait until there's a window of good weather before sending anybody out. Relax, it's ice."

Sean swallowed his wariness and said, "I guess. Hey, call in and let me know if you get picked, though, okay?"

"Okay."

For three days after that, there was no word from Jenny, and Sean began to feel a little better. Chances were she hadn't been picked after all. Then on the fourth day Amanda passed him in the corridor, turned, and said, "Sean! I heard from Jenny today. She tried to reach you but couldn't."

"I've been in the gym," Sean said. "What did she want?"

"She said to tell you she'd been picked and not to worry. She said you'd know what she meant."

Sean swallowed. "Yeah," he said. "I do."

5.2

Relax, **he told himself.** *It will be all right. She's not alone. There are six on the team. They know what they're doing.*

Roger had insisted that things going wrong was the normal state of affairs on Mars, the only thing you could count on.

Sean and Mickey had thought setting up the directional beacon was a snap, a simple job with nothing dangerous about it, and then boulders had begun to rain down around them.

Six people in tents on the plateau of the Daedalia Plain was a reasonable number. Two per tent. If two got in trouble, four were there to help them out.

Still . . .

Sean sat in the quiet school library, studying the largest scale map of Daedalia Planum. It was high country, an immense, uplifted plateau. Parts of it had been overrun with lava flows from the three volcanoes to the northeast, and in satellite photos those areas looked vaguely like reddish colored oatmeal, a jumble of ridges, hills, and blocks of stone frozen in solidified magma. Other parts were sand-covered stone, pitted with impact craters from meteorites. The pipeline was supposed to make its way across these relatively clear areas, avoiding the craters. The rift valley where the water-collection unit had been placed was between Daedalia and Solis, a broad crack in the surface of the planet between the two uplands.

Using a computer, Sean called up a survey set of satellite views showing Daedalia. The craters on its surface seemed to trail dark streaks. Wind streaks, Sean realized. The raised walls of the crater provided wind breaks, and when the storms hit, in the shelter of the wind breaks, the dust and sand collected in teardrop shapes fifty or sixty kilometers or more long. The pictures reminded Sean of the force and power of a Martian sandstorm. For millennia fierce, global hurricanes had roared across the Martian surface, sculpting and eroding mountains, filling the air with impenetrable billows of dust.

Now the atmosphere was thicker than it had been in millions of years, and it would have to be thicker still if humans were going to live permanently on Mars. It was a necessity, but even the weather experts could not predict with any confidence what the heavier blanket of air meant for Martian weather. Generally the storms were fiercest at the time of the equinoxes, the beginning of Martian spring and fall. But the heat of the sun could generate cyclonic updrafts that resulted in awesome blows in summer, too.

And that was just one thing that could go wrong,

Sean knew. He'd read of the history of Martian exploration. Some Earth explorers had died when they plunged through the thin layer of rock and soil over a vast cavern, a gas bubble left over from a volcanic eruption. Others had suffered from rock slides, from earthquakes—Marsquakes, Sean corrected mentally—from the cold, from sudden loss of pressure in buildings and aircraft.

Mars, as Sean had been told over and over, had a million ways of killing a person.

He sat alone and studied the most recent weather images. Nothing alarming. Heavy clouds over the south pole, but that was normal, with the ice meteorites spiraling in and the sun warming the polar cap as summer advanced. The north pole was just the opposite, the carbon dioxide and water ice cap growing rapidly as the northern hemisphere had its winter.

No huge dust storms showed up. There were spatters of lightning storms in the southern hemisphere, another normal feature of Martian weather. Dust clouds generated considerable electricity as the particles spun in the wind, building static charges. Martian lightning storms never produced rain, but there could be fearsome bolts of electricity.

But nothing looked to be an imminent threat. Sean sighed and switched off the computer screen. "Feel better?" asked someone behind him.

Sean jumped and turned, feeling guilty. It was Amanda, sitting at a student work station just behind him. "I didn't hear you come in," he said.

Amanda smiled. "I wondered why you'd been so jumpy for the last few days, and so I decided to ask you. Tracked you down with your wrist locater. Hope you don't mind."

Sean shook his head. The colonists all wore the wristwatchlike devices, tiny transponders that let searchers locate them to within a few meters. It was a surrender of independence, but it was also a safety measure. "I don't know," Sean confessed. "I'm worried about Jenny and her work party. They don't have any heavy trucks, and they're relying on survival tents."

"That shouldn't be a problem," Amanda pointed

out. "It's warm—well, warm for Mars—and they can generate enough air and water to take care of their needs."

"I know," Sean said. He threw his hands up. "I don't know why I'm so worried. It should be okay, but I have a feeling it isn't. Like Roger says, everything goes wrong."

"Sometimes it does," Amanda said. "Sean, Jenny isn't alone. Her team leader is Karl Henried, and he's a level-headed man. She and Alex will have the others to look out for them. Alex is a level-headed young man, and Jenny's no slouch herself. She knows what the dangers are and how to guard against them."

"The people on Earth knew what the dangers were," Sean returned. "They didn't do such a great job of guarding."

"Well, we learn from their mistakes," Amanda said. "I know you have a gift for spotting the weak places in plans, Sean. Is that what's happening now, or is it just that you're lonely and worried?"

Sean had been wondering about that himself. "I just don't know. I'm not even sure how I can recognize trends. It's a feeling more than anything else—the way you can bend a stick just so far and you have the feeling that if you try to bend it just a little more, it will snap. But it doesn't work all the time, and sometimes it's wrong. I hope it's wrong now—or that it's not working at all."

"I hope so too," Amanda said.

5.3

The next morning settled the question. Sean woke up with a sharp feeling of foreboding. He slipped to the foot of his bed and activated his computer, asking it for a weather satellite readout.

The picture flicked to life immediately, live images showing Marsport and the area immediately around it: the southern slopes of Olympus Mons to the north, and the smooth, crater-pocked plain to the south. Sean expanded the view and moved it to the east and to the south.

There. A blurry mass rose over part of the Daedalia

Planum. Sean homed in on it. Not an atmospheric cloud, but a billow of dust. A storm was building—had built overnight—and now was gaining strength rapidly. Sean threw his clothes on and called Amanda. Her face appeared in his viewscreen. "What is it?"

"Dust storm," Sean said. "Big one. Close to the pipeline route on Daedalia. Here, I'll send you the picture." Sean sent it, and on his own viewscreen he saw Amanda's eyes widen in shock as she grasped the extent of the storm.

"The meteorology department said there was a chance of a storm, but they haven't done their daily report yet. That *does* look bad. I'll call the prep party in," Amanda said. "It looks like it's coming in from the north, across the lava flows. Maybe they can outrun it."

It was an electrical storm as well as a sandstorm. Bolts of intense lightning that dwarfed any on Earth shot from the growing, roiling dark cloud, slammed into the Martian surface, shattered and melted rock. Like a gigantic spider, the dark bloated body of the storm rose and stalked across the land on legs of lightning. The discharges interfered with radio communication, and for over an hour Amanda tried without success to raise the advance base.

Sean paced her office, too nervous to sit down, more and more worried as time went on and the storm intensified. Martian meteorologists had a classification system for storms. A ten was a global storm, a blinding, weeks-long rage of wind and sand that blanketed the whole planet. A one was a local storm, a dust devil that could cause minor damage. A two was ten times stronger than that, and a three was a hundred times stronger than a one.

This one, the computer told Sean, had already built up to a four point five. If it had been an Earth hurricane, it would have ranked among the most powerful. A storm that size slamming into the east coast of the United States could rip apart a city the size of Washington.

And if six campers were on the beach with no protection but tents—Sean couldn't stand to think about it.

When Amanda finally got through, the comm tech on the other end said that the station had lost contact with the prep team. "We're okay here, but it's a big one. The pipeline crew have dug in and ought to be safe. We're hoping the prep team saw the storm coming and battened everything down," the tech said, her voice barely audible above the hiss and roar of background static. "If they can get to protection in a crater or behind a ridge, they may be okay."

May be, Sean thought. *May* be.

He went to an auxiliary computer station and called up the current image of the storm. It sprawled over half the Daedalia Planum, a dark mass. Another view showed him lightning strikes. The whole cloud writhed with them.

"Is there anything you can do for the prep team?" Amanda was asking.

"Negative. They're on their own to weather this one."

"Keep trying to raise them," Amanda said. "Let them know we'll get help to them as soon as possible." No reply. She repeated her order and asked, "Did you get that?"

But nothing came back, only the crackle and mutter

of static. The storm had swirled right over the advance base, and it was cutting off communications.

"We've got to send a rescue team," Sean said.

"We'll get a team in as soon as we can," Amanda replied. "I've got the GPS system trying to locate them now. Too much interference, but when the storm lets up a little, we should be able to find them without any trouble. I'm sure they're safe."

"They may not be," Sean insisted. "If the storm hit them before daybreak, it might have ripped all their tents loose. They only had one half-track, and I've seen storms wreck those. We've got to get to them—"

"Sean!" Amanda's voice was sharp. "I know you're worried. But remember, I have to worry about every-one in Marsport, not just about six members of a sur-face team. We operate under a standing order: Never send a rescue team in until they're clear of danger themselves. We can't lose a dozen people trying to save six."

Sean opened his mouth to argue, realized that noth-ing he could say made any difference, and closed his mouth again. Every instinct he had told him that

Amanda was wrong, that waiting meant losing Jenny and the others. Still, he couldn't stack instinct up against Amanda's orders, or against the good of the entire colony.

Daedalia Planum bore the name of the mythical Greek inventor Daedalus, he who had crafted wings to allow his son Icarus and himself to fly. Icarus, though, got caught up in the joy and excitement of flying and had risen too close to the sun. His wings melted and he fell. It had never really happened, of course. It was mythology. Still, Sean could not help remembering that Icarus had died.

Sean left Amanda's office determined that he was going to do something. He might not be able to send a dozen people out to search for six.

But he could send one.

Himself.

CHAPTER 6

Jenny Laslo wondered if she would ever feel that she fit in. The Asimov Project kids had been carefully tested, screened, evaluated, and studied—so why did she sometimes feel that she was the only one of them who had slipped through by accident? Maybe that was why she always tried harder than anyone else, pushed herself to and even beyond the limit.

Sometimes at night she lay awake and wondered if she could stand the strain, and sleep was hard to find. As often as not, she had bad dreams when she did manage to drop off, dreams of her days in an orphanage on Earth, where she was treated as a subject in an ongoing series of experiments. The sense of isolation and helplessness sometimes woke her up with a frightened jerk.

Fortunately, the prep team worked so hard that sleeplessness was unlikely to be a problem. On the first day they had ridden for hours in the little Marscat rover, sometimes having to zig and zag to avoid boulders or ridges. The sun had been too low in the west to let the team do much at the impeller/heating unit, so they had hastily set up the tents and had just called it a day instead.

Just as well, Jenny thought as she and Salma Sauvo wrestled with the fabric-and-metal radiation shielding. The kit was supposed to snap right into shape as a tent. It did, finally, and they set about anchoring it with a hand drill and some rocks. Survival tents had just about enough space to let two people sleep in one, and just about enough heat and oxygen to keep them alive. They weren't much to look at—low, pointed silvery domes, with three tiny round portholes near the top and a bulging flap that was a primitive airlock.

"That's got it," Salma, a dark-haired, dark-eyed Indian woman said, tugging at the last anchor to make sure it was firmly set. "Let's get inside and inflate this thing."

They crawled through the flap, Salma letting Jenny go first. Jenny got inside and said, "Check the outer seal."

"Doing it now. Okay, seal's shut, let me double-check. Right, it's good." Salma wormed her way into the interior of the tent and sealed the inner flap, doing it slowly and taking time to test it. Salma did things by the book, which, she had told Jenny, was the reason she was alive after nearly six years on Mars.

Salma turned to Jenny. Both of them were kneeling because the tent didn't offer much head space for a standing person. "Okay, let's have some light and heat. And a little air would be nice too."

A compact external oxygen generator was already at work, producing a steady, low hiss of incoming air, but the initial tent pressurization came from a small tank of compressed oxygen. Jenny opened it, watched the digital readout on its valve, and when it showed full inflation, she said, "Oxygen's normal." They both removed their helmets.

Jenny had to gasp for air. Normal for a survival tent meant oxygen at a lower partial pressure than in the suits. It was always a bit of an adjustment. Her nose tingled from the cold, and Salma got the small heater going right away. It doubled as a CO_2 scrubber, removing carbon dioxide from the air inside the tent. Without it, the carbon dioxide both of them produced while breathing would build up to dangerous levels. They switched on the tent lantern and unpacked their sleeping bags. "Home sweet home," Salma said with a grunt. "I hope it warms up soon! Check with the others, will you?"

Jenny took the helmet transponder from her own pressure suit. It doubled as a short-range radio. "Tent Three reporting in," she said. "We're set up."

For a few seconds the radio crackled with static, and then Alex Benford's cheerful voice came through the small speaker: "Tent One here. Dr. Henried and I are set up and starting to warm up. Haven't heard from Tent Two yet—but Dales is always slow."

"I heard that!" It was Frank Dales, the electronics expert. "For your information, Joe and I have been comfortably set up for some time. We're just trying to decide what to have for dinner—roast turkey with all the trimmings, or maybe some compressed rations."

"Good idea," Salma said, opening the leg pouch on her pressure suit. "Let's see . . . we have protein bars and carb bars. I'd suggest one of each. Got the water?"

"Right here," said Jenny, hitching the backpack from her suit.

No one could have called it a great meal, or even an adequate one, but the ration bars were packed with enough calories to keep them going and enough vitamins and minerals to keep them healthy. They had just finished when Karl Henried, the team leader, came on the radio to set up the sleep rotation. "Someone needs to be awake at all times to monitor the radio for emergencies," he said. "There are six of us, so ninety-minute shifts will be more than adequate. I suggest that Alex and I take the first two, then Tent Two the next two, and Tent Three the last. Each tent decide who'll take the first watch, and that person will sleep with the radio next to his or her ear."

They turned in at once. Jenny dropped immediately into a deep sleep, without any dreams that she would be able to remember. It seemed she had barely closed her eyes when Salma shook her awake. "Wha?" she muttered.

"It's almost daylight," Salma said. "Your watch. Tonight we'll be waking up in the middle of the night, so get used to it!"

It was cold in the tent. Jenny huddled close to the heater, yawning and stretching her arms. The radio remained obstinately silent. She began to think this excursion was going to be about as dull as the last few days at the extraction station had been.

Breakfast was the same dreary affair as dinner. Jenny munched something that was supposed to remind her of oatmeal with peaches, but it tasted more like someone's old sneaker soaked in peach juice. Everyone took a bathroom break—the tents had chemical toilets, and Jenny had long since gotten over her initial shyness. Modesty was not something you could easily practice in Marsport.

They all suited up and left the tents one at a time. Each time they did, the airlock gave a little puff and a small explosion of vapor shot out—this early in the morning, it froze immediately into glittering crystals. Joe Weston, a pipeline technologist, was last out of Tent Two—a tight squeeze for him. He wasn't fat, but he was the most hammered-down man in the colony—barely five feet four and built like a solid linebacker. Weston was a quiet man, and Jenny had never really gotten to know him. He was always concentrating on some engineering problem.

The sun wasn't high enough yet to provide much warmth. The rusty-red landscape of Mars stretched away into the distance, a rocky surface dusted with fine sand, studded with small rocks and, here and there, a few boulders. Most of these had been blasted out of the crust eons ago by incoming meteorites. A few were ejecta, magma that had been hurled high into the atmosphere from the three Tharsis volcanoes to the north, solidifying and crashing back to Mars again as solid stone. Some of the magma, scientists now knew, had been blasted into outer space during the fiercest eruptions, and a very few meteorites on Earth were actually Mars rocks.

In the early morning the rocks all sent long shadows

streaming across the surface. In the shelter of some of the largest rocks, Jenny could see a fine spiky white frost thrusting out of the dust. It wouldn't have been there a hundred years earlier. Humans were changing the face of Mars, and one of the most vital ways was by making the air denser and, eventually, breathable. Water could exist at the surface now only as ice or vapor, but in time, there would be liquid water on Mars—and eventually, even rain.

"Let's get to work," Dr. Henried said. "Not much scenery to admire here anyway." Jenny blushed and went to help unpack the tool kit.

The heating/impeller station was compact, not quite as large as one of the tents. Months earlier, an advance construction team had dug down into the surface and had set it up, back when the pipeline was supposed to head for the South Pole instead of the rift valley. The prep team tested the unit, switched on its power systems, and made sure the connections were reasonably free of dust and grit. They had to align the microwave dish. This particular unit received most of its power from a direct satellite feed. Its batteries were just meant to provide a buffer against power failure.

By the time the team had finished, the sun had risen almost to the zenith, and the temperature had shot all the way up to a few degrees below freezing. The frost behind the rocks had long since faded away, subliming directly to water vapor without melting first. The sky was milky blue with a high, thin overcast of ice clouds, and the distant sun looked feeble and dim.

They all broke down their tents, repacked them in the side carriers of the Marscat, and climbed aboard for another jouncing, teeth-clacking ride. Henried explained that they wouldn't be able to reach the next unit by nightfall, so they would make camp a few hours away from it. "If it had been a little warmer, I would have said we should make a dash and get to the next unit at about 2100, but there's no sense freezing our feet. There's a small impact crater not too far ahead. I think we should camp in the lee of that. The wind's been kicking up a bit."

Jenny had noticed that the day had turned breezy. Snakes of dust whipped across their path, squirming and slithering as if they were in a hurry to get some-where. She looked off to her right, shading her eyes. To the north, the sky was smudged with high-blown dust, but it didn't look particularly threatening. Any-way, she thought, Marsport or the advance base would give them a call if a storm were developing. Nothing to worry about.

Alex sat beside her. "So, how do you like this?" he asked.

"Better than hanging around in the hootch wait-ing for the engineers to finish rebuilding the extrac-tion unit," Jenny said with a smile. "I don't mind working—it's not having anything to do that drives me zappy."

"I'm trying to talk Glen into letting me take the copilot's seat when we fly back to Marsport," Alex said. He gripped an imaginary control stick. "Techni-cally, I'm a year too young, but I've got more time in simulators than any other pilot in Marsport."

Jenny chuckled. Alex's ambition was to become the best pilot on Mars, and he devoted hours to training. Well, that was understandable. Jenny had always loved animals, and she had decided to become an adaptive agriculturist, finding ways to allow Earth farm animals to function and reproduce in the strange, low-gravity environment of Mars. She put in long hours herself—and she reflected that if anyone had told her three or four years ago that she would almost weep with joy at witnessing the triumphant flight of a chicken, she would have laughed out loud.

Dr. Henried wasn't a very chatty driver, but now and then he pointed out the sights along the way. There weren't many. One part of the plain was pretty much like any other part. At one point they could glimpse the pale bulk of one of the volcanoes far off to the north, almost hidden in the atmospheric haze of distance. They briefly halted near another feature, a tiny impact crater barely five meters across that had been blasted out only ten years before. "Imagine a little space pebble this big," Dr. Henried said, indicating a body a few inches across. "She comes whistling in from somewhere out toward Jupiter, almost vertically. Boom! She hits and vaporizes in an explosion that blasts out a hole like this. Lucky for us one hasn't smashed into Marsport, eh?"

Alex and Jenny exchanged a glance, and Alex gave her a wry smile. It was just one more way that Mars could kill you. There were so many, Alex's smile seemed to say, that one more didn't make much difference. Still, Jenny resisted an urge to look upward, as if something big and deadly might be hurtling their way at that very instant.

6.3

They arrived at a much larger impact crater not long before sundown. This one was far older, and it had been made by a far larger meteorite. The crater was more than ten kilometers in diameter, and they were heading for its southern side. The blast had thrust up a crater rim that looked like a curving range of hills forty meters high. Once they might have been jagged, but centuries of wind had ground them down into rolling, rounded shapes.

The wind was steady from the north, so they planned to camp on the sheltered south side of the crater. Even with the thin air of Mars, a strong wind could damage a survival tent.

But it meant a colder night. South of the equator, the north side of the crater got the most direct sunlight. When they scrambled off the Marscat and began to unpack the tents, the crater's shadow was already deep, and the temperature was plummeting. There were a few advantages. The wind shadow of the crater was a collecting ground for the fine Martian dust, and the portable oxygen generators worked very efficiently with that material. On the other hand, it was hard to stake the tents down through a meter of dust, and the job took so long that by the time they finally got into the tents, stars already glittered in a rapidly darkening sky.

Jenny slept dreamlessly again, and this time when Salma shook her, she didn't complain.

"All quiet?" Jenny asked.

"Except for the wind."

Jenny heard it then, the scratchy hiss of sand against

the outside of the tent. She shivered. If it was this bad behind the shelter of the crater rim, the wind must be howling out in the open. But they'd had no word of storms. Maybe it was just a seasonal thing.

She kept her ninety-minute watch, then called Alex in Tent One to wake him for his turn. He sounded foggy, as if he had been snoozing deeply, and she kept him on for a minute to make sure he was fully awake. "Are you up?" she asked in a soft voice, not wanting to wake Salma.

"Yeah, yeah," Alex grumbled. "Anything happening?"

"Windy."

Alex was silent for a moment, and then he said, "Yeah, I hear it. Sounds pretty fierce. Think I should wake Dr. Henried?"

"Probably not. It'll be dawn in three hours, and you'll get him up in an hour and a half anyway. Let him sleep, unless it gets worse. It's been steady ever since I woke up."

"Okay. Grab another few hours of sleep. I'm awake now, I promise."

Sleep didn't come, though. Jenny lay awake listening to the sifting-sand sound of the wind, wondering if it were growing stronger or staying about the same. It was hard to tell. She was still awake when Dr. Henried gave out the general call, and she tapped Salma's shoulder. "Still blowing," her tent-mate said. "Hope it's not working into a storm."

After breakfast, all six of them got out of the tents. Jenny knew they wouldn't be going anywhere the moment she looked around. A few hundred meters to the west, beyond the shelter of the crater rim, the air was a blurry rush of dust and sand. Even in the protected area, they walked in a kind of reddish fog, a fog made up of microscopic dust particles whirling and blowing in eddies of wind. Jenny could make out the shapes of the others, but she couldn't tell the tall, thin Henried from the short, heavyset Weston in the swirling gloom.

"This isn't good," Dr. Henried said. "Luckily, we can hold out for a week if we have to, and this should blow over well before then. But we'd better head west for a while, to get to the center of the crater's protection. I doubt we can raise the base by radio with all this going on, but let's make some tracks and we'll try."

They rode for a couple of hours, with visibility dwindling the entire way. Finally, Dr. Henried stopped the vehicle. "I'm going to foul the bearings if we keep rolling in this," he said. "Let me get the blade in place, and I'll see if we can scrape down closer to bedrock."

The Marscat could double as a scraper with its blade swung out from its slot under the cab and locked into position. Henried jockeyed it back and forth, digging a gradually deepening trench in the drifted sand. He excavated a strip ten meters wide and thirty or so long, finally stopping when the cat blade began to snag on rock. "That will have to do. Get the tents up."

With the brickdust fog growing thicker, it was hard work, but at last they all had their tents ready. "Meeting in Tent One," Henried said.

A survival tent was never meant to contain six people. They were elbow to elbow, sitting on the floor. Dr.

Henried looked worried. "All right. Let me give you just the skin." Jenny leaned forward. *The skin* meant the most important facts, the essentials. Dr. Henried continued: "We're off the trail, folks. Normally we would have gone around the north side of the crater, but we need the protection, so I made a decision to divert. However, that means that advance base won't know where to look for us—and until the wind dies down and I can aim a microwave dish at a satellite relay, I can't raise them on the radio. We'll hunker down here for at least a day to see if this is going to get any better. If it doesn't, we'll think of a contingency plan. Everyone get some rest and conserve your food and water. They may have to last us for a long time."

Jenny nodded. She felt nervous, but not especially afraid—not until she noticed how scared Alex looked. Alex was a rock. If he was frightened, there was something to be scared of.

That was when she first began to think that they might not make it back.

CHAPTER 7

"Okay," Sean said to Roger and Mickey, his voice low and conspiratorial. "First, what I want to do is against all the rules, so we could get in trouble. I don't have anyone's permission for what I'm going to try. You need to know that up front."

Mickey's plump face was solemn, his eyes sharp behind his spectacle lenses. He and Roger exchanged a glance, but neither of them spoke. Then Mickey tilted his head and asked, "How much trouble?"

Sean shook his head. "I just don't know. Dr. Simak won't send a rescue team out to look for Jenny and the others, because she doesn't want to risk any more lives. I want to go myself, but I can't go alone. I don't have Dr. Simak's orders or even her permission, so if I'm caught, I'm in for it. I need help."

The three of them were in Sean's room, Roger

sitting backward on the computer chair, Mickey lounging against the wall beside the door, Sean sitting on his bed, which was folded into its sofa position. Sean leaned forward, his arms resting on his knees, his hands clasped. He studied the other two boys, but their expressions told him nothing.

Roger frowned and held up a hand as if asking for silence. "Now, let me see if I understand you, Sean. Correct me if I'm wrong in any of this. You want us to go with you out into a dangerous storm and try to find the prep team, right? If we succeed, we'll be in terrible trouble with the council, and if we fail, we'll probably all die? Is that pretty much it, then?"

"Pretty much," Sean confessed.

"Oh, right, then. I'm in." With a carefree smile, Roger leaned back with his hands clasped behind his head, as if he had made his decision and was comfortable with it.

"Are you jumping ahead too far? I mean, wouldn't the Advance Base have sent out a rescue party already?" Mickey asked, sounding undecided.

"Not likely," Sean told him. "They're catching the

brunt of the storm. It's worse there than it is on the trail, from the satellite pics. We're clear of the storm's path here, so we can move before anyone from Advance Base can. We have to get to Daedalia Planum and—"

"Hold on, hold on," Mickey said irritably. "Ax the plans for a minute, will you, and let me catch up? First, how are we supposed to get there, with the storm and all? They're a long way off. I suppose we could take a hauler and carry enough spare fuel to make it, but it would take weeks to get that far, and by then they'd be back, or—well, it would be too late."

"We can't make it by land. We have to fly," Sean said. "That's the only way."

Mickey stared at him, then took off his glasses and polished them. "Fly. Into an electrical storm. Right. And what do we do when the wings rip off the plane? Flap our arms and hope for the best?"

"We can't take a plane," Sean said. "So we take a ballistic shuttle."

"Oh, a rocket," Roger said, nodding solemnly. "Sure, that would work like a charm. He's got you there, Mickey. Now it all makes perfect sense."

"It does," Sean insisted. "In a shuttle we can arc in above the atmosphere, so the storm won't matter. We'll put the shuttle in VSTOL mode and pick a place to set down that's sheltered, or a place where the storm has already passed. If we take a Series One, we'll have the surface rover for transportation after we land."

"A Series One shuttle?" Mickey asked, putting his glasses back on and looking suspiciously at Sean. "Pretty tall order for just the three of us, Sean. Those babies are designed to go into orbit and return. So who's supposed to fly this thing?"

"I can't, and Roger can't," Sean said.

Roger laughed. "Well, that narrows it down a bit, I must say. Mickey, I know you've flown planes, or at least that you've sat in the copilot's seat while someone else was flying them. How much shuttle time do you have? Any at all, or is this going to be a case of on-the-job training?"

"I made two trips as copilot while the *Argosy* was offloading cargo," Mickey said, shaking his head.

"And I've put in about twenty hours on a simulator. I've never made a takeoff or a landing solo. With the computer assist the Series One has, I probably could do it, but it's taking a big chance. Anyway, how are we supposed to get our hands on a Series One?"

"They're not guarded or anything," Sean pointed out. "Hangar One is full of pipeline equipment, and the shuttle that was to ferry some of it down was already out on the revetment and partly fueled when the storm blew up. It's sitting there waiting for us, just wrapped in plastic. If we miss the chance, we'll have to wait until the next cargo ship from Earth arrives— lots of shuttles will be available then."

"But there won't be one of those for a while," Roger said. "And it would be too late for the surface party then too. Come on, Mickey. I've got enough electronics to know how to help. Once you get us off the ground, I can set the nav computer, and it's pretty much tending the baby after that. The thing practically flies itself."

"There's the little matter of landing."

Sean shrugged. "The Series One does a vertical

descent and set-down. In fact, Giles Tallant told me he set one down in a crater a few years back when he had to make an emergency landing."

"Giles Tallant helped to *design* the Series Ones," Mickey pointed out. "And he's probably the best shuttle pilot on the planet."

"You can do it," Roger insisted. "Look, even I've made VSTOL landings on the simulator. It's easier than a runway landing. Just takes fuel, that's all."

"I don't know. Maybe. Tell me about this storm," Mickey said.

Sean shooed Roger from his seat and used the computer to call up satellite images. "Here it is. Lots of lightning discharge, as you can see. It's a big one bearing southeast, but the northern edge has already swept past Arsai Mons," he said, pointing out the spot. "The prep team is somewhere in this area, south-southeast of Arsai. By the time we get there, the storm should be clearing."

"We can't get too close to the storm. Winds can really mess up a vertical landing. And we'll have to monitor the satellite feed to make sure the storm isn't changing direction or firing back up," Mickey grunted. He whistled. "Man, look at that. It stretches all the way south to Tierra Sirenum. That's a big blow."

"And Jenny's out in it," Sean said.

Mickey didn't reply right away. Roger said, "Come on, Mickey. You're the wizard at everything you try. Anyway, what's the worst they can do to us, assuming we even survive? Send us back to Earth? Not bloody likely!"

"I ought to have my head examined," Mickey complained. "You know I'll catch most of the grief for this, because I'm the oldest. Okay, let's hear your plan."

Sean leaned forward and started to explain, occasionally turning to punch up a display on the computer. He called up a large-scale relief map of the area and indicated a series of red dots. "These are the stations the team had to prep," he explained. "When the storm hit, we know they had already serviced the first one. We got no readings from the second station— either they never reached it, or the storm disrupted communications before the report came in. Anyway, we need to check out the second station to see if they reached it. If not, then we have to backtrack. The trail is marked with directional beacons, so that shouldn't be a problem. They ought to be somewhere on a line between the second station and the first."

"All right," Mickey said. "It's crazy, it's zazzy, but we might be able to pull it off. When do we go?"

"As soon as we can. Now."

"It's the middle of the night!"

"Then no one will see us, will they?" Roger asked, standing up.

Mickey seemed to have no answer for that. Of course, Sean knew, someone would see them. But if they had any sort of luck, they'd be seen as the shuttle lifted off, and by then it would be too late for anyone to stop them.

With any sort of luck, Sean repeated to himself.

7.2

The wind had been bad, but the lightning was worse. Jenny flinched every time they heard the sizzle of a bolt, and the strange thunder of Mars, tinny and high-pitched in the thin atmosphere, vibrated in her skull. The small porthole windows in the tent turned a brilliant blue-white every time a lightning bolt struck, and she could almost taste the acrid ozone.

The constant sizzle of sand on the tent made conversation all but impossible. She and Salma sat hunched on the floor of the tent, close together, their helmets on their knees. The tent was holding, so far, and the anchors were keeping it in place. There was no telling what the lightning was doing to the electronics on which they depended. Even a near miss could fry the circuitry inside an oxygen generator— or, for that matter, inside the Marscat.

Jenny closed her eyes as another lightning bolt slammed into the surface somewhere not so far away. The rock beneath the tent vibrated from the discharge. "The hills," Salma said, and the rest of her sentence was lost in the roar of the storm.

Scooting closer to her, Jenny yelled, "What?"

Salma shouted into her ear. "The hills will attract most of the lightning. It hits the highest point."

Jenny nodded and hoped that was true. The crater

rim had been there a long time, and storms had hit it often enough before. Jenny had explored a similar crater rim once. She remembered how the rounded stone hills had strange scoops taken out of them, round or oval depressions meters across. Lightning scars, someone had told her. A bolt of electricity the size that you got in a Martian electrical storm could shatter stone, or melt it in a nanosecond. If one of those hit the tent, well, she and Salma would never know it. Jenny shivered. What would it be like? An explosion of white light, then nothing? Would she even have time to know what was happening?

Maybe not, if she was lucky.

She felt the radio transponder vibrating in her helmet and pulled it out, pressing it against her ear. "Tent Three here," she yelled as loudly as she could.

Scratchy static poured out of the receiver, and under that, Alex's voice, broken up so that only a few words came through: ". . . suits. Losing . . . to get to . . . be ready."

"What? What?" Jenny felt like shaking the radio. "Alex, I didn't get that. Say again. Say again!"

Static. Then, suddenly, "Coming in!"

Jenny guessed what was about to happen. "Get your helmet on!" she yelled to Salma, and she put hers on.

Salma followed suit, just in time. The inner seal of the airlock gave way, and with a gust that she felt rather than heard, the tent lost its air pressure. Alex scrambled in and turned to seal the inner flap. He said something that Jenny couldn't hear—she hadn't replaced her transponder. She held it up and shook her head.

Alex nodded. He checked the seal, then repressurized the tent. He took off his helmet, and so did Jenny and Salma. Alex shouted, "Our tent ripped! Lost pressure fast—lucky we had our helmets ready. Tent's wrecked, but we're okay, and I brought our oxygen tank. Dr. Henried's in Tent Two. I can't get the outer seal to fasten-dust in the seam. Keep your helmets ready. If the inside seal blows, you're going to need them."

Jenny turned her gaze toward the flap, feeling sick at the thought of a blowout. Normally, the tent exit was like that of an igloo—a tight fabric tunnel, with one airtight seal opening into the tent, one out to Mars. If the outer seal was open, then nothing stood between them and suffocation except the inner seal, bulging outward from the pressure of the air in the tent, pulled at by the near vacuum of the Martian surface. How much could it take?

Salma was yelling something that the constant cascade of sound drowned out. Jenny leaned close to hear. ". . . your helmets. I may be able to get it to seal."

"We'll lose oxygen!" Jenny said, realizing what Salma was about to try. "Too dangerous!"

"I'll be all right," Salma insisted. "Alex, hold my legs. The oxygen rushing out may clear the dust from the seal, but I don't want it to blow me right out into the storm."

Jenny put her radio back inside the helmet and cringed as another bolt of lightning came uncomfortably close, making the receiver squeal like a wounded animal. She got her helmet in place and watched as Salma unsealed the flap.

The pent-up air whooshed out of the tent again, and Salma wormed through the opening on her stomach. Alex held her ankles as she writhed and twisted, muttering to herself. Her worried voice crackled over the transponder, but Jenny couldn't make out what she was saying—probably a string of curses, she guessed. Then Salma spoke more distinctly: "I see where it's fouled. If I just had a silicone cloth, I could—let me try this. Okay, okay, it's sealing. Got it! Not perfect, but within tolerances. Watch out, Alex, I'm coming back."

She pulled herself back into the tent, resealed the inner flap, and said, "Pressurize."

Alex did, keeping a critical eye on the oxygen readout. "Not much left in your tank," he said.

"We've got yours," Salma told him. "If the generator holds, we should be good for a few days."

"How long can this thing go on?" Alex asked.

"Not much longer," Salma said, but Jenny thought she sounded as if she didn't believe her own words.

Marsport never slept. Someone was always on duty, and even late at night it was hard to get through the entire installation without someone seeing them. Roger knew where the cameras were, though, and they worked out a tortuous route that would get them to the hangars before they'd be likely to be spotted. "No help for it once we're in the hangar," Roger said. "If we're lucky, no one will be paying attention to the monitors. I hope there aren't any burglar alarms."

"I never heard of any," Mickey muttered. Sean thought the older boy looked as if he were regretting his decision. "Look, the only Series One that's fueled will be the one that was set to ferry pipeline materials to the advance party. It's equipped with a cat, but the storm blew up before it was fully fueled. It'll be taking a big chance."

"Too bad they didn't get lost when the *Argosy* was here," Roger observed. "All the shuttles were in use then."

Sean nodded. When Marsport had lost touch with Earth, 176 colonists had decided to return to Earth orbit aboard the *Argosy,* one of two interplanetary ships that had kept the colony supplied. Now, months later, those colonists were still somewhere in space, spiraling in toward Earth and whatever awaited them there. The Asimov Project kids had narrowly escaped being aboard it—only through a defiance of the rules had they remained behind.

And now here he was breaking the rules again. Sean tried not to think about what Amanda would say. He only hoped he'd be alive to hear it, no matter how angry she would be.

"Okay," he said. "We go through the Lake Ares dome, then through the greenhouses. I know them pretty well. No surveillance cameras there. Then we'll take the service corridor to the hauler garage, and then we go out on the surface to get to the hangars."

It was the only way. The corridors leading from the colony to the aircraft hangars were locked, and they had no time to steal the codes to get through them. On the other hand, Sean reflected, it was the unexpected way. No one walked around on the surface at night.

They got into the lake dome with no trouble. Sean felt his throat tighten. This was Jenny's favorite spot. He could see that the lake was down some. It was almost perfectly round, occupying a crater that the colonists had domed over. The lights in the dome were at minimum power, giving just a dim illumination. The surface of Lake Ares lay as smooth as ice, without a visible ripple. Sean sniffed. The air smelled, somehow, of water. It was homelike, reassuring.

The greenhouses were bathed in a dim red light, infrared, keeping the plants at a safe temperature. "Warm," Mickey mumbled.

"Smells nice," Roger said. "My mum and dad used to do a lot of gardening when they were home."

Sean didn't say anything. Roger's mother and father had been doctors, and they had been killed by people they were trying to help in one of Earth's senseless little wars. Roger didn't often speak of them, but when he, did his voice always lost its light, joking edge and sounded older, regretful, strained.

It seemed to take them forever to go through the string of greenhouses. The last few were cold, not yet planted. "Better suit up here," Sean said as they approached the hatch that led out of the last one. "The garage isn't pressurized, and it'll be awkward trying to get into these helmets and packs in the corridor."

They were wearing their blue pressure suits, but now they donned the helmets and helped one another with the backpacks. "Good to go," Mickey said. "Look, I'll lead the way, all right? If we get caught, they'll think this is my idea anyway."

"No, they'll probably think it's me playing a practical joke," Roger said. "Wish I could think of a funny one right now."

They went through a long passageway, partly constructed, partly dug through bedrock. The door at the end bore a red marker: It had direct access to the surface of Mars. Mickey operated the airlock, and the three of them crowded into a space about the size of a small closet. The hatch closed behind them, air circulated out, and then Mickey opened the outer door.

Strange, Sean thought, that not so far away a storm was raging. Here the night sky was achingly clear. One of Mars's two tiny moons was high in the sky, hardly more than a bright smudge of light too big to be a star. Sean thought it was probably the potato-shaped, deeply cratered Phobos, whose slow orbit gave viewers the illusion that it moved from west to east.

"Hope everyone went to the loo," Roger said as they stepped out onto the hard, bare rock of the landing field. "We're not stopping along the way."

Sean didn't reply. A few work lights gave them some illumination, and their shadows stretched out weirdly. They hustled to the hangar with the ski-like motions of Martian running. Mickey was breathing hard when they got to the access hatch. "Okay," he said. "I've got the code to get us in. The shuttle should be in position near the hangar doors. Roger, you'll code in the override to get the hatch open. They'll know something's going on then. You'll have about ten seconds to get aboard, and then we'll have to go. Everyone clear?"

"Clear," Sean and Roger said in unison.

They opened the hatch and stepped out onto the surface. Near an enormous hangar, the shuttle, a conical craft with stubby wings, pointed up to the night sky. A plastic bubble covered it, mildly pressurized and attached to the marscrete revetment by a pressure ring. Roger knelt by the ring and said, "These things are forever malfunctioning. If we're lucky, the tower will read this as just another minor blowout. Here we go."

Roger opened a small hatch and tapped a control panel. The ring released, and the flexible plastic shot off the base with an inaudible *whoosh.*

"Get aboard," Sean said, leaping up onto the revetment and using his transponder to activate the boarding ladder.

A hatch slipped smoothly open in the side of the craft, and the ladder slid to the ground. Both boys scrambled up it.

Mickey hurried forward. He got into the pilot's seat, powered up, and leaned past Sean to wave at Roger. "Here goes," he said through clenched teeth. "I'm activating the emergency liftoff program on the autopilot. They'll know something's up as soon as I do. Hang on tight."

Sean fastened his seat restraints as Roger clambered into the navigator's station directly behind him. "Let's go, let's go," Roger said tersely.

Mickey was working at the control panel. "Power's at full. Lay in our course, Roger. I'm shutting off the radio. There's nothing they can say that we want to hear."

Roger fumbled at his station. "Hang on, I haven't got it connected yet."

"Just feed it the memory stick," Mickey said. "Sean, brace yourself. This is going to be rough. Here we go!"

The craft began to shudder as the engines engaged. The lights on the landing field flared. Someone knew that a ship was about to take off, and in a minute they would be coming out to ask questions.

"Trajectory is in," Roger yelled. "Go, go, go!"

Sean gripped the arms of his seat. Mickey threw a final switch. "Power to the engines," he said, and the craft began to move. "Anything, Sean?"

"Don't see anyone yet. Wait, there's a Marscat coming out of the garage, two people in it."

"Too late," Mickey said. "We're off."

The shuttle leaped into the air, gaining speed, and then Mickey yelled for Sean to grab the stick. They both pulled back as the shuttle hit airspeed, and Sean felt the g-forces building.

Outside the cockpit, Mars fell away. The lights of Marsport slipped behind them, and then the planet was a dark shape in the dark night. Sean had never seen anything look more deserted.

"We've done it," Mickey growled. "We got away. Now you guys can cheer."

"Hooray," Roger said mildly. "This is exciting, I must say. I almost hope we live."

CHAPTER 8

The wind finally began to blow itself out before dawn. The sun rose, sending red-tinged shafts of light through the portholes of the tent. Jenny stood stiffly and peered through one. She might as well have tried to stare through an aluminum plate. The sand had scored and scratched even the resistant plastic until it was opaque.

"Sounds better, anyway," Alex said. He took his transponder out and keyed it. "Tent Two, this is Tent Three. Do you hear me?"

Dr. Henried replied almost at once: "Tent Two here. We're okay. How are you doing?"

Alex said, "Well, we're cold and hungry, but we've got air. At least for now. I don't think our generator's working."

Jenny realized then that she wasn't hearing the reassuring hiss of incoming oxygen. She felt a rising panic, like a tide of cold water washing over her stomach and chest.

"Probably buried and fouled," Henried said. "We've a spare one in the cat, and we can always use the one from Tent One. Let's have a council of war. Your tent or ours?"

They agreed to meet in Tent Two. Salma led the way out. The morning was still, but incredibly hazy—fine particles of dust would be suspended for days or weeks after a blow like that one. Jenny groaned when she saw the wreckage of Tent One. The side facing the blow had developed a rip, and fingers of wind had widened it, shredding the tough pressure-resistant fabric. The tent was partially buried in a drift, and partially unraveled in a long, jagged ribbon that snaked over the fresh fall of dust. They had to scoop sand away from the airlock of Tent Two before they could unseal it and make their way in, one at a time.

Jenny followed Salma in, and Alex came behind her. Dr. Henried was looking tired and worried. "Right," he said. "Well, we have the two tents, anyway. We should be all right if we run straight back to Advance

Base. I expect they'll have a team out looking for us as soon as they can, so we'll probably run into them. Now, we're about sixty kilometers south of where we should be, so the first thing to do is set up the microwave relay and get word to them. Let's eat, and then we'll go home."

They had a fairly cheerful meal, considering. When they had finished, they took small sips of water. "Might as well conserve it," Henried said. "We can't pick up any more out here."

They dug out Tent Three and found the oxygen generator ruined. Something, maybe dust getting into the circuitry, maybe a surge from a lightning strike, had fused its electronics. The generator from Tent One seemed to be all right, though.

The Marscat had taken a pounding. The flying sand had scoured all the paint from its metal surfaces, and they gleamed as if they had been polished on purpose. Henried got the portable microwave dish out and set it up, but after a few minutes of trying, he said, "No good. Circuits are fried. Help me dig out the cat, and we'll make a run for it."

The front of the cat had vanished into a crescent dune of dust and sand. They scooped it away, repacked the tents, and climbed aboard.

It was too quiet. After a minute, Jenny asked, "What's wrong?"

"Can't get any power from the cells," Dr. Henried said. "Lightning, I suppose. And I'm not going to be able to repair this with what we've got on hand. Ladies and gentlemen, I'm afraid we're going to have to walk out of here."

Walk? Jenny closed her eyes. They had been thirty kilometers south of the trail when they first went south of the crater. And they wouldn't be able to walk straight across the crater—they'd have to follow its rim. Thirty kilometers was more than eighteen miles. Add to that the distance they had traveled to get to the shelter of the crater—what? Maybe twenty miles total?

The pressure suits were good for four hours before their oxygen had to be recharged. Could they make five miles an hour? Probably not, even in the low gravity of Mars. They'd have to take oxygen with them.

And the tents—could they haul the tents with them? That would slow them up, but without the tents, they'd face a Martian night exposed to the cold and the winds.

Dr. Henried was talking again. "We can break down the sides of the cat and fashion a travois. We'll put one of the tents on it, and all the supplies. We ought to be able to make fifteen kilometers by sunset, and we'll get an early start tomorrow. Let's get to work."

It took them hours. By the time they had lashed together the crude sledge, the sun was halfway up the sky, though it was visible only as an orange smudge in a rose-colored murk. They recharged their suits and began the long walk, taking turns hauling the travois behind them. They had rigged a couple of crude skids, but even so towing the sledge was a constant irritation. It snagged on rocks, it tilted and wobbled constantly as they went up or down hill, and it dragged at them, slowing them to a crawl. On the treadmill, Jenny could manage a steady 6.4 kilometers per hour. She doubted that they were doing half that.

The sand under their boots was yielding, flowing,

slippery, making them stumble and lurch. Dust collected on their faceplates, and they had to wipe it off time and time again just to have some vague idea of where they were going. Noon came and went. The sun sank, fading as it lost itself in thicker layers of drifting dust. They struggled along in a murky half light, resting for ten minutes out of every hour.

Henried called a halt at last. "I estimate we've done at least fifteen kilometers," he said. "Let's pitch camp and get what sleep we can. We'll need to start early tomorrow."

They were all staggering with exhaustion. Setting up the tent was excruciating, and once they had all crowded in, finding enough space to sleep seemed an impossibility. Jenny hunkered near the inner flap, and Alex slumped beside her, his face drained.

"Cheer up," she told him. "We ought to reach the trail tomorrow, if nothing else goes wrong."

With a weak smile, Alex said, "It could be worse, I guess. I can't think how, but there must be some way."

Jenny laughed, though she didn't feel like it. It was either that or cry.

The shuttle angled down just as the sun cleared the eastern horizon. "Find us a smooth place," Mickey said. "That's all I want, a nice, firm, smooth place to set her down."

"Scanning with the radar," Roger said, sounding absorbed in the task.

Sean sat in the copilot's seat itching to do something—anything—but not able to help. He didn't have the piloting skills of Mickey or the computer knowledge of Roger. It was frustrating to admit, but all he could do at the moment was trust the others. "Storm's moving to the southeast," Roger said. "Okay, we're due north of the second station. Let me see . . . there's a little hill with a big trail of dust behind it, but if we set down here, we should be okay. Will we be able to take off again?"

"In VSTOL mode, sure," Mickey said. "But after that, we can set down only once and take off only once and still have enough fuel to get back to Marsport. If we have to do any more landings, we're out of luck. We'll never make it back."

"But we can call for help," Sean said. "If we find them, we can call for help."

"If I crack this crate up, we can call for help," Mickey added. "If we're still alive to do it. Okay, I'm turning nav over to you. Sean, sit back and don't touch anything. If we're lucky we'll come down in one piece."

The landscape of Mars rose alarmingly fast. Sean gripped the arms of the copilot's seat and had to remind himself to breathe. Vague blotches rounded into craters, their eastern depths in shadow, their western sides lit by the rising sun. What looked like pepper sprinkled on red sandpaper suddenly became boulders strewn over a broadly flat plain with a few dunes and rolling hills. Then the ship's engines swiveled, the thrust kicked at Sean, and they settled toward the surface. Clouds of dust rose as the ship came down, and it crunched in with a very solid sound.

"Are we okay?" Roger asked in a shaky voice.

"Checking," Mickey said. "Engines shut down.

Fuel's okay, attitude's okay. We're down, the ship is level, and I think we can take off again. Now what?"

"Now we break out the cat and visit the station," Sean said.

8.3

Six kilometers to the south they found it, marked by a beacon that had been twisted into a corkscrew by the wind. Sean opened the hatch and checked inside. "Not activated," he said. "They didn't get this far."

They shuffled back through billowy ankle-deep sand to the cat. Visibility was less than a kilometer—the fine red dust still hung in curtains. Roger turned on the directional finder, though, and it showed another beacon somewhere ahead. "About five clicks," Roger said. "The trail marker."

"They'll be on the trail," Sean said. "I think we should take the cat a few markers down. We'll probably see them. They can't be far off."

"Call the Advance Base," Mickey said. "See if they've heard from them."

"They'll yell at us."

Roger switched on the microwave relay. "I've been yelled at lots of times."

They got nothing, no signal at all. "What's happened at Advance Base?" Roger asked, sounding both concerned and fearful. "You don't think they're all—"

"The lightning," Mickey said quickly. "It's fouled up their transmitter, that's all. You saw the weather readouts. They had the worst of the storm. May take them days to get back online."

Sean hoped he was right.

They made slow time. Driving the cat in that strange red mist was almost like driving blind. Roger called out the directions, but every other minute they had to divert around boulders, and once or twice rolling crescent dunes defeated them, sand and dust piled high but too loosely packed and unstable for them to drive across. They had to go around, and guessing which side of the dune offered the best path led them into some labyrinths. From time to time Roger sent out a hailing call on the prep team's emergency frequency, but without any response.

The second beacon was nearly buried in a drift. They saw no sign that anyone had been there, and they headed toward the next beacon, another five clicks down the trail. "What's around here?" Mickey asked. "What geographical features?"

Areological, Sean corrected mentally, but he said nothing out loud and studied the map. "Not much. There's an impact crater ahead and to the south."

"Big one?"

"Ten or twelve kilometers across. It has an eroded rim that's elevated well above the plain." Sean strained to see ahead. "We're not going to fall into it."

"I think you're drifting too far north," Roger said, bent over the navigation console. "Bear to the right a little more. That's good. What's our speed?"

Mickey sniffed. "About three clicks an hour."

"These things can do thirty."

Mickey's face was red with frustration. "You try doing thirty in this mess!"

"All right, all right," Roger said. "I know you're doing your pathetic best."

Mickey didn't answer, but he did speed up. They

reached the next marker, stopped, and repeated their call.

"Nothing," Mickey said. "If it was clear, we could do a flyover and look for—"

"Hold on!" Roger's voice was sharp with concern. "I heard something. Boost the gain."

Sean adjusted the radio, straining his ears. Crackling static, a constant hiss. And then—words? He couldn't be sure. Maybe. Maybe.

Roger said, "I don't think that's anyone calling us. More like pressure-suit radios. They're talking to one another, and we're barely able to pick up a signal, but it's too weak for us to make it out."

"Where are they?" Sean asked, pounding his fist on his knee.

"Hang on, I'm trying to get a fix." Roger muttered under his breath, not to Mickey or Sean, but just begging whoever it was to keep talking. Sean felt as if he wanted to leap out of the cat and go running across the surface of Mars, but he fought the feeling down. He couldn't hope to find anyone on his own.

From the electronic mush, Alex's voice came suddenly

sharp for a couple of words—"don't let"—and then it was gone again. Roger said, "This can't be right. They wouldn't be twenty kilometers southeast of us, would they?"

Sean fumbled frantically with the map. He found the location of the nearby beacon, giving him their spot on the map, and then he measured twenty kilometers. "That would put them way south of the trail. Twenty clicks, let's see, that's a spot just inside the crater wall. No way would they go in there!"

"Or maybe they're just *outside* the crater if the fix isn't just right," Mickey said. "How could they get so far off the trail?"

"Don't know," Sean said. "Look, we have to go on and check this out. We can make it in four hours."

"Maybe," Mickey said. "But we can't make it back to the shuttle before nightfall."

"We've got a survival tent aboard," Roger said. "If we find them, we can crowd together with some in the tent and some in the cab of the cat. Shouldn't be too hard to get through one night."

"I don't like leaving the shuttle," Mickey said.

"No one's likely to steal it," Roger pointed out.

"No," Mickey replied, controlled anger in his voice. "But what if another storm comes up? What if the shuttle got hit with lightning or buried in a drift?"

"Then we'd take the cat to Advance Base," Sean said.

Mickey shook his head. "What if we find them and take them to Advance Base and—and things aren't right there? What's the plan then?"

"Don't ask so many what-if questions," Sean said. "None of that has happened yet, and we can't be sure it will happen. But we know Alex is out there somewhere, and we know he's talking to at least one other person. If we head back to the shuttle, we'll lose the trace. I say we go on."

"We have to, Mickey," Roger said. "Seriously. What if it was you out there?"

Mickey let out a long breath. "I suppose I'd want some loonies to come looking for me. Okay. Sean, look sharp and keep me from driving this thing into a gulley. We have to make tracks."

They wound their way forward slowly, taking a

twisting path around obstacles in their way. Sean kept checking the weather photos, but as far as he could tell, the storm was heading southeast now, away from them—though he could tell from the high-resolution images that the area around Advance Base had been hard hit. The radio chatter came and went, never clear enough to understand. They tried broadcasting on the same frequency, but they couldn't be sure if they were getting through. Each time they heard something like voices, though, Roger worked to refine his radio fix.

"Helmet radios are generally good over line-of-sight distances of four kilometers or less," he said once. "If we can get around this bloody big pile of rubble"—he glared at the rim of the crater, passing by on their right, looking like a dim wall in the poor afternoon light—"we should be able to talk to them."

"Why aren't they using their cat's radio?" Mickey asked, but it was a question none of them could answer.

They drove on in uneasy silence, all of them staring ahead. Sean, at least, was a little fearful of what they might see, but Roger was right: They really had no choice but to follow the ghostly voices and hope for the best.

The oxygen generator failed fifteen minutes after they made camp. Dales went out and brought it into the tent, but they couldn't find the reason for the breakdown. Apparently some circuits had been fried by the lightning, but they had no way of testing the unit and no way of repairing the circuits.

"That's pretty grim," Salma said. "How much tanked oxygen do we have left for the tent?"

"Tonight," Dr. Henried said. "That's it. But I suggest we wear our suits and save the last of the tent cylinder. It can give us another three hours of oxygen apiece."

Jenny did some quick mental calculation. With the oxygen tanks they had dragged behind them on the travois, the suits had a forty-hour supply. Advance Base was more than two hundred kilometers away to the east. At the most, they could probably make three kilometers an hour, two hundred and forty kilometers . . . eighty hours.

Alex seemed to read her thoughts. "Don't worry about running out of air. We'll find the trail. Advance will send a team out to find us, and they'll be equipped with everything we need. We're not dead yet."

"Of course not," Salma said, putting a hand on Jenny's shoulder. "Not by a long shot."

They had an hour or so of oxygen left in the tent before they had to put the helmets on. As far as it was possible in the cramped space, Dr. Henried, Dr. Dales, and Dr. Weston got together and carried on a quiet consultation apart from the other three.

At last, Dr. Henried cleared his throat. "We've come to a decision," he said. "We'll make for the trail and try to get as close to Advance Base as we can. If it seems possible that a party will not be able to save us all, the three of us will give whatever remains of our oxygen to you three."

Salma objected at once. "No. That's not fair. None

of the women-and-children-first nonsense. We're in this together."

"True," Dr. Henried said. "However, if some of us must die so that some of us can live, well, that's the only logical course to follow. Far better for three of us to survive than none."

"Then we draw straws," Salma said. "I won't play by your rules."

Jenny looked at Alex. He seemed to be struggling, but he finally said, "I agree."

Jenny was truly afraid now. But from somewhere she found just enough courage to say, "So do I."

9.1

The afternoon was rapidly losing itself in a murk the color of brick dust. Mickey had turned on the cat's headlights, but they were little help. The airborne dust turned the beams into a blurry glow that hardly made a difference in visibility. "We should be able to get through to them," Sean said for the seventh or eighth time.

"It's this bloody dust," Roger returned. "It's diffusing the signal the same way it's diffusing the headlamps. We have to be close, though. Five clicks or less, I'd say."

"It'll be night soon," Mickey muttered. "Then what?"

"We have to keep going," Sean said. "We'll be okay in the cat."

"Yeah, until I topple us off a scarp or crash into a boulder," Mickey replied. "Sean, it's too dangerous.

Nobody goes rolling across Mars at night, even in good weather."

"Shut up, shut up," Roger said frantically. He had clapped headphones over his ears, and he leaned forward, eyes squeezed closed, concentrating. "I can make out some words. I hear a man, Alex, and—yes, it's her, it's Jenny! I'm going to try to get through again. Obviously they haven't heard us yet. Stop the cat, Mickey. I'm going to see if I can send them a directional beam. Maybe that'll get through this soup."

It was frustrating work. A narrowcast radio beam was more powerful than a broadcast one, but it had to be aimed just right in order to get through. They had rounded the northeastern side of the crater, and they assumed that the people they were looking for were almost due south of them. "Almost" wasn't precise enough, though. Roger spoke into the radio: "Prep Team, this is a rescue team. If you hear me, respond."

No answer, after three repetitions. Roger adjusted the directional antenna fractionally—a matter of a few centimeters here meant that five clicks away the beam could be half a kilometer to the right or left. He repeated his call. Then another adjustment, another repetition. Sean felt his stomach fluttering as if he'd swallowed a flock of butterflies. They were so close. Why couldn't they make contact? He itched to take the radio controls from Roger, but he knew that the younger boy had expertise he lacked.

"Come on, come on," Sean said under his breath, urging Roger to keep trying and Jenny to answer him.

The sixth try. The seventh. And then, just as Roger was about to move the antenna again, a man's voice, just on the edge of hearing: "Say again? Rescue team? This is Prep Team. Where are you?"

Mickey exhaled loudly, and Sean realized he had been holding his breath too. Roger handed the receiver to Sean. "You're the boss. Tell him."

"Prep Team, this is a rescue team from Marsport," Sean said. "We can't get a good GPS fix because of the after-effects of the storm. We believe we're a few kilometers north of you."

"Who is this?"

Sean looked at the others. "Sean Doe," he said. "I'm, uh, the rescue team leader."

"Henried here. Who's the senior member of the rescue team?"

"Mick—uh, Michael Goldberg," Sean replied. "But I'm the one responsible."

Sean heard two yelps of surprise, and Jenny said, "Sean! What are you—"

But Henried shushed her and said, "Are there no adults on the team?"

"Give me that," Mickey said. He took the receiver and said, "Dr. Henried, the important thing is that we've got transportation if you need it, along with medical supplies, food, and oxygen. Give us your situation."

A long pause, and then Henried said, "We're in a bad way. Our cat's broken down, and though we're all right for food and water, we've only a few hours supply of oxygen. No casualties, but we're all pretty much exhausted. Under the circumstances, I won't ask too many questions. It's good to hear a voice, no matter who it is. What can we do to help?"

Roger took the receiver back again. "I need a better fix on your position," he said. "Do you have a directional transmitter?"

They didn't. But Henried had a good idea of the team's location with respect to the crater—he said they were just off the two o'clock position, maybe a hundred meters east of the crater rim.

"Got it," Sean said. "We're coming as fast as we can, but visibility is bad. It'll be full night before we can get there. We could drive right past you in the dark."

"I think we may be able to help with that," Dr. Henried said.

9.2

Alex stood outside the survival tent. He wondered how cold it was. Fifty below, at least, and the temperature was plummeting. Like deserts on Earth, Mars gained heat during the sunlight hours but lost it rapidly at night. Alex had been outside the tent for half an hour, and he wouldn't be able to stand much more. He held a work light at his chest, a brilliant halogen lamp that in ordinary circumstances could provide illumination for a huge area. He pointed it north, but for all its brightness he couldn't see anything much. The dust scattered the light, giving him the impression that he was at the bottom of a murky, blood-colored sea.

His feet were beginning to feel like icicles. He'd have to give up and go inside the tent in a few minutes, and then it would be someone else's turn. "You're still coming, aren't you?" he asked over his helmet radio.

Sean's voice came back at him, as clearly as though they were standing next to each other: "We're coming, Alex. It's slow going. We're making about a kilometer an hour. Just can't see anything more than three meters ahead."

"I'm holding up the brightest light on the planet."

"We're looking for it, buddy. Hang tight. We can't be too far away."

Alex stamped his feet. Maybe he could take it for a few more minutes, he thought. He'd count to five thousand. Slowly.

He was past three thousand when he saw a shape. Alex held his breath. Had he been fooled by a boulder? No, he saw a light now, a pair of lights—the cat's headlights! He let out a whoop.

"What was that?" It was Dr. Henried, his voice sounding strained to the breaking point.

"I see them!" Alex waved his lamp frantically. "Guys, I see you! I'm off to your left. Turn ten degrees to your left, and you'll be coming dead at us!"

"Got you!" It was Sean. "I can see your light now. Hang on. We'll be there in a minute or two!"

Behind Alex, the tent flap opened, and they all came creeping out, from Dr. Henried to Jenny. They stood behind him in a loose group, all of them staring at the approaching lights. "I thought we'd had it, to tell you the truth," Dr. Henried said in a conversational tone.

"I should have known Sean would think of something," Jenny replied. "He's like that."

"I heard you," Sean's voice said over Alex's helmet radio. "Mickey says to tell you we expect you all to testify at our trial."

Alex grinned, but then he reflected that Sean wasn't that far off the mark. Something was very suspect about the rescue mission. There might not be a trial, exactly, but there would be a world of trouble.

The cat came to a vibrating halt a few yards away. After fifteen seconds or so, the cab airlock cycled and a pressure-suited figure dropped out and onto the surface of Mars. Whoever it was came stumbling forward in a run. "It's so good to see you!" the figure yelled, and the voice was Sean's.

Jenny jumped forward to meet him, hugged him clumsily, and said, "Whatever happens, *I'll* testify for you."

"Thanks," Sean said. "We may need it."

9.3

The next morning they piled into the cat, a tight fit, and went bumping along back toward the shuttle. The day was much clearer, with only a misty hint of the dust haze that had been such a problem. Now that he could see, Mickey got more speed out of the vehicle. Sean didn't know whether Mickey was relieved to see the shuttle still resting sound and whole, but he was.

Dr. Henried led the way into the shuttle. The bay, built for cargo, was spacious enough for them all to gather without crowding. "Very well," he said. "I propose this: Salma is certified as a shuttle pilot, so she'll take command of the Series One and fly you three, plus Alex and Jenny, back to Marsport. Dales, Weston, and I will take the cat, a microwave set, food, water, and oxygen and return to Advance Base. We'll call for help if there's anything we can't handle."

"All right," Sean said.

Dr. Henried stared at him. "Young man, I wasn't asking for your agreement. I was simply giving you orders."

Sean felt something inside him wither. Amanda's stare, he thought, was going to be just as cold as that, and her voice just as formal. It was almost enough to make him wish that he didn't have to return.

Salma checked out the shuttle systems, found them all in working order, and started to plot a course back to Marsport. Roger coughed and said, "I've already done it. You can check my work if you wish, of course."

Salma did, and then looked up with a faint smile. "Good work, Smith. Perfect, in fact."

"Thank you." Roger gave an embarrassed shrug.

Dr. Henried and the other two men set out at about two in the afternoon, and shortly after that Salma lifted the shuttle off the plain. Mickey sat beside her in the copilot's seat, and Roger was still at the nav station directly behind him. Alex, Sean, and Jenny were in passenger seats.

The flight back seemed too short to Sean. One minute they had cleared the boulder-strewn plain, the next the nose of the shuttle was tilting sharply up, and then, only seconds later, they angled in for the approach and landing. He'd had hardly any time to talk to Jenny.

Well, he'd had hours, if you counted them up. But somehow he couldn't find words to say or the will to say them.

The sun was low in the west when the shuttle taxied into its hangar and the clamshell doors closed behind them. They all suited up and left the shuttle, heading through a corridor into one of the arrival bays.

Sean swallowed hard as he took off his helmet and stepped into the bay. They had a reception committee. Amanda was there, looking far from pleased.

But worst of all was the expression on Dr. Ellman's face.

It was a satisfied, malevolent smile.

CHAPTER 10

"Do you have anything to say for yourself? Look at me, Sean."

Sean was staring at his toes. At least Amanda had taken him to her apartment for the chewing-out, he thought. She could have done it in her office, in front of Ellman and the others. "No," he muttered.

"Look at me," she repeated.

Sean's eyes felt hot. He forced himself to lift his gaze to Amanda's face. Her expression was stern and unforgiving. And sad, Sean thought. She looked as if he had hurt her beyond words. "Now. Have you anything to say?"

He cleared his throat. "We found them," he said. "I think everyone should remember that they were lost and in trouble and we found them."

"Of course you did," Amanda said, her eyes not softening a bit. "But you left the station without permission, you risked your own lives, and you risked a shuttle that we have no way of replacing. You broke the rules."

"Sometimes . . . ," Sean began, and then trailed off.

"Sit down, Sean," Amanda said. Her apartment was no more spacious than his room, and he sat on the folded sofa-bed. She sat in the other chair, facing him. "You have put me into a very bad position, Sean. I'm the executive of the colony, and I have to have the loyalty and the confidence of everyone on the planet. Do you see what you've done?"

Sean's throat was almost too tight to let the words out. "I saved my friends' lives. You'd do the same. I know you would. If it had been me out there—"

"Sean. Listen to me. We're on a planet that can kill us in a second. I am responsible for more than three thousand lives. I have to think in terms of keeping all of those people safe, or if I can't do that, of keeping as many as possible safe. When you took the shuttle, you took the only way we had of reaching Advance Base in less than a day. It was the only shuttle fueled and ready to go. What if we'd received a distress call? What would we have done?"

"I don't know," Sean admitted. He said, "Could I ask you something?"

"What?"

"Have you heard from Advance Base?"

Finally, finally, Amanda's expression became less forbidding. "Yes. They're safe. They lost communications because of the lightning, but there was no serious damage. When Dr. Henried gets there, he'll find everything is in order."

"Then we did the right thing," Sean said.

Amanda shook her head. "No. My point is that we had no way of knowing, Sean. Before you go to rescue six people, you must think of the eighteen others who may be in danger in another place. You have leadership skills, Sean, and I respect that. But a leader has a terrible burden to bear, and it's called responsibility." She sighed. "You think that if you had been lost instead of Jenny and Alex, I'd have done the same thing. I know that I would have been tempted, but I'd have had to make the call according to my best judgment. Sean, you have to know that if you were in danger and eighteen other people were in equal danger, I'd have to try to help them first. I'd *have* to. And if it were the other way around, if you could save me or save a half-dozen other colonists, you'd have to let me go and do what's best for the whole colony. Those are the rules we have to live by on a new world."

Sean nodded. "All right. What's my punishment?"

For the first time Amanda smiled. "You are a problem. You really are. Yes, you saved the lives of six people, and everyone knows that. However, I can't let you off with a reprimand or a warning. Everyone knows you're my legal ward, and I can't show favoritism, not as a leader. The council will hold a hearing. You can present your side of the story, and they'll consider your testimony. But you will have to pay for your misjudgment in some way."

"Who's going to be the judge?" Sean asked.

"It isn't a trial," Amanda said. "But Dr. Ellman will preside."

Wonderful, Sean thought. Of all the people on Mars, the one whom Sean had ticked off the most was Dr. Harold Ellman. He remembered how Ellman had raged against the Asimov Project, how he had argued so strongly that children had no place on Mars. And he recalled all the sarcastic speeches Ellman had given him. Even when he had earned the man's praise, it had been given grudgingly.

If there ever was a hanging judge, Sean told himself, *I'm about to face one. Wonderful. Just wonderful.*

"It was my idea all along," Sean told the three council members who were considering his case. "I talked Mickey and Roger into going because I couldn't do it without their help. They only came because I persuaded them."

Dr. Ellman sat at the front of the classroom flanked by Tim Mpondo and Graciela Platas. Ellman leaned forward and asked, "Did they consider that they were breaking regulations? Defying a direct order?"

"Jenny and Alex are our friends," Sean began. "They—"

"Please answer the question, Doe," Ellman snapped.

"You are a very bright young man in class. I know that you can answer a question when you choose."

Sean bit back angry words. They were useless—they'd only get him into even more trouble. "We talked about it," he said. "But we decided—"

"You knew you were doing wrong," Ellman said flatly.

Tim Mpondo's dark face was unreadable, but in a kind voice, he said, "Dr. Ellman, I believe Sean was offering an explanation. I would like to hear it."

"Go on," Ellman said.

Sean couldn't look directly at him. He kept his eyes focused just over Ellman's head. "Sir, we decided that we had to take the chance to save the lives of our friends. And of the others who were missing. That's all."

"And you did save them," Mpondo commented. "We've heard from Dr. Henried. Advance Base had no way of communicating with them and was dealing with severe problems of its own. They had sent no rescue team out and probably couldn't have sent one for another forty-eight hours. By then it would have been too late."

"Yes, sir," Sean said.

Dr. Platas had her hands on the table before her, fingers linked. "So," she said slowly, "we have to balance the saving of six lives against your admitted disobedience. That's what it comes down to in the end."

"Yes," Sean said again.

Dr. Ellman looked at the two council members. "Anything else?"

Neither of them said anything. "Very well. Doe, do you have anything to add?"

Sean thought for a moment. "We risked our three lives to save six lives," he said slowly. "I know we all could have died. But we're all alive, and I think that should count for something. I don't think you should punish Mickey and Roger. I talked them into it. I'll take whatever punishment you decide, but they're not to blame."

Silence, and then Ellman said, "Is that all?"

"Yes, sir."

"Then you are dismissed. You can wait in the computer room."

Sean turned. Behind him, Mickey and Roger sat at a

table, their faces tense. They got up, and the three of them left the classroom.

Alex and Jenny had both testified, and they were waiting outside. "What did they say?" Jenny asked.

Sean shook his head. "Don't know yet."

"Well," Roger said thoughtfully, "at least we don't have any guillotines on Mars. I think Ellman would just as soon chop our heads off as not."

"We're sunk," Mickey said. "They're going to do something horrible to us. I can feel it."

"They can't," Alex protested. "Man, you three are *heroes.* There'd be a revolt if they tried something bad."

"I think we're only heroes to a few people," Sean admitted. "To everyone else, we're rule-breakers and troublemakers."

"Anyway," Roger put in, "we'll have to wait and see."

10.3

Waiting was as hard as anything Sean had ever done in his life. An hour went by, and another, with no word from the council. "They should have made up their minds by now," he said.

Roger was playing chess against himself on the computer and losing both ways, as he often said. "Probably trying to decide how long we'll survive on nothing but bread and water."

"Or disqualifying us from our specialties," Mickey said. "That's what worries me. I've trained for so long. If they won't let me be certified, what am I going to do?"

Roger didn't look up from his game. "You could always—"

The door opened, cutting him off. Roger jumped up from the console, his face deathly pale.

It was Dr. Platas. "Come on," she said. "We've reached a decision."

They sat at the table across from the three council members. Dr. Ellman tented his fingers and gazed at the three young men with a certain cool detachment that made Sean's heart sink. For perhaps half a minute he simply stared at them. Mickey stirred uneasily, and Roger was jiggling his feet nervously.

Finally, Dr. Ellman said, "We have to admit that some good came out of your, ah, escapade. In all likelihood, the Prep Team would have perished if you had not broken the rules to go after them. However, we can't be certain of that. Because you took the only available shuttle, the authorities at Marsport could not launch a proper rescue effort. We have to consider that, too."

He took a deep breath. "Against the admitted good you've done, you have all three broken the rules of Marsport. I don't know whether to congratulate you or censure you, Mr. Doe. You are once again first in an endeavor. We've never had to have a trial in the colony before. Perhaps it is fortunate for you and your friends that we don't have a brig or a prison wing—at least not yet."

Mickey groaned softly, and Roger sat frozen, no longer drumming his heels. *Here it comes,* Sean thought.

Dr. Ellman said, "We have to administer some form of punishment. You are lucky that we are in a struggle for survival, and that we care for your education. It is the decision of this hearing that you will continue in your schooling and in your work assignments. However, for the next three months, you will be confined to your quarters at all times you are not in school or working at your assigned jobs. That is all."

Sean dared to breathe again. All? He could hardly keep from laughing. The council had just sentenced the three of them to sleep in their own rooms—that's what it amounted to. *Well,* he amended mentally, *we'll lose weekends, but still, it's only for three months. I can live with that.*

"However," Dr. Ellman continued, "Mr. Doe, you were the ringleader. The council agrees with me that your situation calls for somewhat harsher measures." He nodded, and Lt. Mpondo rose, went to the wall, and opened a storage compartment. Inside hung a blue Pathfinder pressure suit. Sean swallowed, recognizing the number on the helmet as his own.

Dr. Ellman said, "We are revoking your surface privileges for six months, Mr. Doe. This suit is no longer yours. You will not be allowed to check out even an Excursion suit. You will be allowed only a standard yellow emergency decompression suit with a thirty-minute oxygen supply. That is all."

The three council members got to their feet, and Mickey, Sean, and Roger rose too. Mickey said, "Thank you, Dr. Ellman, Lt. Mpondo, Dr. Platas."

A beat later, Roger also stammered his thanks. Sean muttered something too, but his heart wasn't in it. He thought of the other Asimov Project kids in their blue Pathfinder suits, and his heart sank. Ellman had done it. He had found a way to set Sean apart from the others, a way to take him right out of the team. This was going to hurt.

CHAPTER 11

A month later, Sean had almost changed his mind. It wasn't that very much was different. As he had first thought, for five days out of every week his punishment was little more than having to sleep in his own room. But he found that he missed the free time. Being stuck in his room for two days out of the week, eating his meals there, reading and studying, and trying to entertain himself, got old fast.

Worse was his loss of surface privileges. Worst of all, perhaps, was the way the others tried so hard not to mention their trips out of the domes. Sean sometimes felt that he had a horrible disease and the others didn't want to mention it.

Still, he got to see Jenny during class times. She was happy that the colony was at last getting a more than adequate supply of water. Lake Ares was safe for the next ten or twelve years, anyway. And then—well, as

Jenny put it, water was coming in to the South Pole every day. In ten years, who knows? Perhaps the atmosphere would let surface water exist. They might get rain, or at least fog. That was something.

A step forward, Sean thought. *What's that old Earth saying about a long journey beginning with a single step?* They were on a journey to the future, one that had brought them 35,000,000 miles. Every step moved them a bit farther along.

Sean wasn't completely lonely. He, Roger, and Mickey could visit one another during their confinement to quarters, and as often as not the other guys would hang around the dorm wing to keep them company. And he could visit Amanda, though it was some weeks before he got up the nerve to do that.

When at last he did, they went for a walk. Sean had no idea what Amanda was up to—she led him through work stations, through the library, through recreation areas. People spoke to him, and he responded. Most of them had smiles for him and encouragement:

"Way to go."

"Hang in."

"Three months will be over before you know it."

Back at Amanda's apartment, she asked, "Have you been thinking over our last conversation?"

"Yeah. I mean yes," Sean said. "I see what you mean."

"Most people we passed today seem to admire you."

Sean shrugged. "But they know I broke the rules."

"They know you're paying for that too." Amanda leaned forward. "Sean, it's good to have the respect and the admiration of people. It's better to earn it. And it's best of all to be willing to risk that if you have to make an unpopular decision, but one that you know is right."

"I know," Sean said. "I'm sorry." He felt miserable. "All my life I've wanted to belong somewhere. I couldn't have let my friends die. I had to do something. I'm sorry for what I did, but I'd do it again."

"Well, honesty is a virtue," Amanda said. "I'm sorry, too. I'm proud of you, Sean . . . son. I'm very proud of you."

They sat and talked for hours. It was a time that Sean was to remember often in times to come.

It was a time when he felt that he truly belonged.

OUTCAST

#1 The Un-Magician

by Christopher Golden & Thomas E. Sniegoski

TIMOTHY IS A FREAK, a weakling, an impossibility. He's the only person in existence without magical powers and has spent his entire life hidden on a remote island.

When Timothy is finally taken back to the city of his birth, he finds he is marked for death. Assassins are watching his every move, and the government wants him destroyed. Timothy can't imagine what threat he could possibly pose; after all, he wields no power in this world.

Or does he?

The OutCast quartet begins August 2004

Aladdin Paperbacks • Simon & Schuster Children's Publishing Division
www.simonsayskids.com